"*Confluence* is a slow burn. It teems with perfectly selected details and multi-layered dialogue to create extraordinary tension that climaxes in unexpected ways. I can't remember when I've become so fully immersed in fiction."
—KEN HARVEY, author of *The Book of Casey Adair*

"A powerful novel—simply and directly told, with a great narrative engine and a fully realized emotional arc."
—TREVOR CORKUM, author of *Here with You*

"In Wade and Teddy, Turner and Childs have created two boys caught between instinct and fear, loyalty and self-preservation. *Confluence* is a powerful coming-of-age novel about masculinity, repression, and the devastating consequences of love that cannot safely speak its name."
—DANNY RAMADAN, author of *The Foghorn Echoes*

Confluence

ARSENAL PULP PRESS
VANCOUVER

Confluence

a novel

ALEX TURNER
& LUCIAN CHILDS

CONFLUENCE

ARSENAL PULP PRESS
Suite 202 – 211 East Georgia St.
Vancouver, BC V6A 1Z6
Canada
arsenalpulp.com

The publisher gratefully acknowledges the support of the Canada Council for the Arts and the British Columbia Arts Council for its publishing program and the Government of Canada and the Government of British Columbia (through the Book Publishing Tax Credit Program) for its publishing activities.

BRITISH COLUMBIA | BRITISH COLUMBIA ARTS COUNCIL An agency of the Province of British Columbia | Canada Council for the Arts Conseil des arts du Canada | Canadä

Arsenal Pulp Press acknowledges the xʷməθkʷəy̓əm (Musqueam), Sḵwx̱wú7mesh (Squamish), and səlilwətaɬ (Tsleil-Waututh) Nations, custodians of the traditional, ancestral, and unceded territories where our office is located. We pay respect to their histories, traditions, and continuous living cultures and commit to accountability, respectful relations, and friendship.

Arsenal Pulp Press is committed to reducing the consumption of nonrenewable resources in the making of our books wherever possible. We make every effort to use materials that support a sustainable future. This book is printed on paper made with 100 percent sustainable recycled fibre content.

This is a work of fiction. Any resemblance of characters to persons either living or deceased is purely coincidental.

The following chapters were previously published in different form:
"All We Have" in *The New Quarterly* 179 (2026); "Before the Revolution" (originally titled "Sea Change") in *Prairie Fire* 46, no. 2 (2025).

EU Safety Regulations authorized representative: Easy Access System Europe, Mustamäe tee 50, 10621 Tallinn, Estonia, gpsr.requests@easproject.com.

Cover and text design by Jazmin Welch
Cover photo: *Alex and Vern Barber at the Beach* (detail), Vancouver, BC, 1959. Photographer unknown. Courtesy of Lucian Childs.
Title spread photo: *Chilliwack-Sardis Overpass* (detail), Chilliwack, BC, 2002. Photograph by Alex Turner. Courtesy of Lucian Childs.
Photo on page 198: Courtesy of Lucian Childs.
Edited by JC Cham
Proofread by Alison Strobel

Printed and bound in Canada

Library and Archives Canada Cataloguing in Publication:
Title: Confluence : a novel / Alex Turner & Lucian Childs.
Names: Turner, Alex, 1940–2019, author. | Childs, Lucian, author.
Identifiers: Canadiana (print) 20260135100 | Canadiana (ebook) 20260135151 | ISBN 9781834050416 (softcover) | ISBN 9781834050430 (EPUB)
Subjects: LCGFT: Novels.
Classification: LCC PS8639.U7617 C66 2026 | DDC C813/.6—dc23

For
Marjorie, Patricia, Sam, Bess,

and

Alex,
always

Part 1

I remember what it was like … to be young, *very* young …
When everything, touching and tasting—everything—
was so new, and even suffering was wonderful
because it was so complete.
—JAMES BALDWIN, *Another Country*

dancing the logs

THAT MORNING WE met by the river, it was 1956. Middle of May, probably, since I recall the maples were leafed out, but the air retained the previous night's chill. Not a school day, I think. I remember our classes—as always at that season—seemed incapable of ever coming to an end. I was fourteen, that's certain, and, judging by all those photos Mother took of me that year, I was pale, sporting the crewcut of the day, and already tall, rail thin. My body muscular but lacking the bulk and definition I later worked so hard to acquire.

Tattered bathing shorts ballooning around my toothpick legs, a towel looped over one shoulder, I barged through head-high salal to scurry up a ridge bounding the Harrison River. Under the sheltering limbs of fir, hemlock, and cedar, my tennis shoes negotiated a trail latticed with tree roots—an obstacle course I'd long since mapped into memory.

Just then, the sun peeked out of its hiding place behind the Lillooets, its light strafing across the lake to project swirling yellow and crimson banners in the mist that threaded the tall trunks. It was as if I were suddenly in one of the great churches of England, whose photos I'd seen in the school library's encyclopedia, sunlight from high arched windows streaming through columns onto rows of the devout.

As I halted on the trail to admire this beauty, the sun arced behind a cloud and the light show winked out. It was replaced by the laughter I had hoped to dodge—the boastful, mocking tones of other teenage boys. My shoulders tracked upward. My jaw tensed as I scrambled on all fours up the basalt outcrop to the crest of the ridge. There, parting a thick stand of huckleberry, I peered down at the mouth of the river.

At the bottom of a stony embankment where a log boom was anchored, six or so boys from school rushed onto the slick timbers, taunting, grappling, shoving one another into the cold water. A broad-shouldered boy in a white-belted bathing suit—his thick limbs teetering at his sides—spun a sun-bleached trunk with his bare feet until he lost his balance and spilled into the icy bath.

Everybody else wore swimsuits or sported cut-off jeans—but not him.

He had stripped down to white briefs. Hauling himself out of the river, they clung to his buttocks, translucent in the sun. With the light glistening off his compact and muscled frame, his skin startlingly pale, for a moment it seemed as if the world around him had blurred. Everything erased but him.

He lurched to his feet, water cascading down his body. Speeding across the boom, he flew from one sinking trunk to another—his arms outstretched, his fingers splayed—dancing the logs.

I headed for a spot on the bank far enough from the others to be out of their line of fire. I stashed my towel, waded from shore, and climbed onto the boom. Scrambling to its far rim, I dove in. The cold shocked me, and I surfaced gasping, kicking.

I struggled to find a hold on a slippery log and managed to clamber back on, only to slide once again into the frigid water. Surfacing, I flipped onto my back, kicked up spray that showered me with prisms of refracted sunlight.

I snuck glances at the boys through the stubborn strands of mist still hugging the water's surface. I'd spied on them for years. Watched them high up in the trees, passing around cigarettes in their private fort. A couple of them caught me slinking underneath it once and pulled down their pants to piss a steady stream, calling out together in girlish voices, "Yoo-hoo, Teddy Bear."

That morning, though, only my log dancer discovered me staring. He paused on the tree trunk he spun, teetered there, his head cocked, taking me in. Now, I wonder if this was our wordless communication, already growing between us. But then, I jerked my head away, gazed behind him at the boom cobbled together in sections, the timber stretching a quarter mile downriver. Waiting for a tug to tow it to one of the sawmills that lined the Fraser.

Feigning indifference, I dog-paddled around and faced east. There, the clear, glacier-fed waters of Harrison Lake began their short course down the river to the muddy confluence with the Fraser. Nearby lay our village, Harrison Hot Springs, named after the sulphur and potassium cauldron that boils at the southern end of the lake.

At this time of year, the lake and river are completely ours. Summers, though, the area teems with tourists from provinces all round—even the States—swimming in the goose-pimpling water, taking in the sights, soaking in the hot pools at the resort where my father then worked as a groundskeeper.

Into the wilds to the north, the lake stretches some forty-five miles between two mountain chains. Only a few miles wide at most. A drowned valley; any closer to the coast and it would be a fjord. Or inlet. Or sound. Sound. I liked that best, could imagine on fogged-in nights and days the ghostly horns sending out warnings from the big ships in Vancouver Harbour.

A deadhead, a nearby log partially submerged and angling out of the water, drifted downstream. I pictured it escaping the Harrison River—merging with the swift-moving Fraser and reaching the Pacific, beyond these mountain barriers—if it didn't get swamped or beached along the way.

I decided to swim for it. The farther I side-stroked from the boom, the more the reflections of sky and clouds patterned the river's surface. Intermingled among them were the greens and yellows of the mountain on the opposite shore. I was mesmerized as their edges grew blurred and indistinct, fragmenting and swirling when I disturbed the water.

Shouting startled me. I heard my name called faintly. "Teddy!"

I cast about for where the boom should have been, only to find the rapidly scrolling screen of forest. More shouting and I squinted upriver to spot pale distant arms waving me back.

I attempted a stroke in their direction, but my limbs had numbed. My dead weight dragged me under the chilly water. Sunlight pierced the mottled blue above—so enthralling, those shimmering rays of vivid green that enveloped me. Again, that sacred slant world of silence and beauty. A refuge from the arena of ordinary boys, their bullying and hateful jibes.

But past those bright columns, within a vortex that drew me toward the murky depths, flashed a sinister presence, like the monster under the bed I'd feared as a child. And at that sight, an electric sensation surged through me. A sudden intake of water. A panicked thrashing of arms and legs, labouring against that darkness.

I breached the river's surface yelling, snorting water and phlegm. My arms plowed into the current, and the colourful patterns shattered. There was only my gasping breath, the aching in my limbs. The voice in my head urging me: *Don't stop don't stop don't stop.*

Exhausted when I reached the safety of the cove, I wriggled onto the edge of the boom farthest downriver. My lungs heaving, I crumpled onto my stomach on a wide smooth log and attempted to slow my breathing. Sun dried my skin, tightening it. Waves lapped against my log, its gentle bobbing soothing me. Under the pride I felt—for proving my physical strength, for being alive still—in my body's lingering chill, that feeling of dread I'd experienced moments before remained.

Through eyes still smarting from the cold, the glare off the river, I noticed the log dancer running toward me. He leapt by, dripping, his arms juggling the air for balance, thighs tense, feet controlling the timber. As if in slow motion, he sprang out of, then back into my line of vision. Abruptly he halted, seemingly in mid-air, turned, then duckwalked to where I was lying.

"You okay?" Head tilted, he was staring at me hard, brows furrowed.

I propped myself up on my forearms to speak to him. Silhouetted against the sky, the curve of his shoulders was outlined by the morning sun.

"Yeah, I'm just out of breath is all," I said.

"You were way out there. Didn't know if you'd hear."

"That was you yelling? How'd you know my name?"

He shrugged, gazed downriver. "That's a far swim. Saw you driftin'. Current coulda swept you off."

Legs astride, he was balancing on the ends of two logs, shifting his weight, submerging one, then the other. I tried not to glance at his cock, contracted from the cold, a little knob pulsing against wet underwear in rhythm to his movements.

"I ... just wasn't paying attention," I said. "I was looking at the colours. In the water."

He peered over me at the river. "Colours? You mean, like, all that blue?"

"Well, yeah, but more. Greens. Yellows. Reflections from the mountains. Clouds too. They get all mixed up. You see them best when you swim out."

Slowing his see-sawing motion, he considered me for a moment. "Yeah, I guess. If you say so. Sure looks blue to me." He hopped onto my log, and as it adjusted to our combined weight, I clung to its sides, careful my fingers weren't pinched by the adjacent floater.

"What I do see out there is a seal," he said.

"A seal? Where?"

He pointed to a dun-coloured shape drifting near the far shore, a speck, not unlike my deadhead that was disappearing downstream. "See them when I swim across sometimes. They come up the Fraser from the ocean, then the Harrison to the lake. Old man finds plenty too around camp."

"Your dad's a logger?"

He smacked his thigh, marking the pale skin in red but missing the zigzagging horsefly that hovered there, attempting another landing. "Sonofabitch is a tree faller up at Thirty Mile. Me and Mom, we used to live up there. But there's no school, no nothin'. So we rent a piddly house in Harrison now. Dad comes down by mail boat every couple of weeks to cause a ruckus. These here are from his camp. You can tell by that mark." He motioned to the sawn ends of the logs corralled in the boom. Then without warning he leaned down and slapped my shoulder.

"Hey!"

"Sorry. Didn't mean to hurt you," he said. "Horsefly. Almost got him. They'll take a big old chunk out of you if you let 'em." He stroked his hand across his chest, then up his neck to the beautiful thin line of his lips. "Got any smokes?"

I shook my head no.

"Be right back."

He darted over the timber to the edge of the boom, leapt ashore, then rummaged through a pile of clothes. Most of the kids had gone back to town or were climbing the cliffs beyond the trail. A few were still lolling on the logs or sitting there talking. Pop music of the day—Elvis, Everly Brothers, maybe—was borne faintly on the air from their transistor radio. The log dancer gave them a wave, and I figured he would return to socializing with them. Instead, he skipped back along the shifting trunks with a lit cigarette.

"Where'd you learn that?" I said.

"What, smoking?"

"No. Running over logs. Without falling in."

"Watchin' the guys at camp." He eyeballed our boom and related how the watermen corralled the timber. Chaining it together, manoeuvring in heavy spiked boots. Fast, so the logs didn't sink under their weight. He paused and pulled on the cigarette a few times, billowing smoke out his nostrils.

"Dangerous work. Just the other week, one guy drowned. Real experienced too, my old man said he was. Still, the guy slipped through the boom, and it closed over him. They had to jimmy the thing open to get at the corpse." He glanced over as if hoping to find me properly impressed. "A boom man, that's what I wanted to be. Once."

Leaning down, he poked his cigarette between my lips, his fingers grazing my mouth. I flinched at his touch, so unaccustomed was I to the easy physicality of other males. I marvelled too at the familiarity with which he dealt with me, so unlike the remove from people I'd cultivated over the years.

He squatted directly in front of me. Then, balancing on his hands, he slowly lowered himself to straddle the log, legs dangling loosely in the water. Easing a hand under his briefs, he made a speedy adjustment.

After inhaling the cigarette—slowly, so I didn't cough—I passed it back to him. The smoke left me feeling woozy. And as he turned his attention first to the cigarette, then back to me, I wished myself bold enough to gape at the wisps of hair nestled between the arcs of his chest. Instead, I held my focus on his face—his hazel eyes topped by the dark line of his crewcut.

He twisted around to eye a couple of boys goofing at the far end of the boom. "Fucking idiots," he laughed, though his face appeared scornful, a little sad.

"What, don't you like them?"

"I guess, but they're stupid as all get-out. Not one decent thought between the bunch of them."

While he was scowling at the boys, I freed my eyes to snatch a quick line down his chest and abdomen, to linger a beat on pubes showing through damp white cotton, before my gaze darted, finally, to the safety of the bobbing timber. It was all I could manage, during those instants when the attention of the boys I desired was drawn away, as if I were a spy scouting among the enemy.

He flicked the cigarette into the air, and I tracked its trajectory until it fizzled in the water.

"I see you around," he said. "At school, in town. Your face in a book, mostly. What are you? Grade 7 or somethin'?"

"Nine, actually."

When I returned my gaze to him, I realized he was studying me. It was the first he appeared guarded. My stomach tightened, my breath hitched until he blinked and a smile washed across his face.

"Lucky son of a gun," he said. "Did you skip a grade or something?"

"No. Why?"

"I mean, you look kinda young."

The old shame crept over me; because of my baby face I was always being taken for a little kid. I exhaled, tried to deepen my breathing, but I was way too tense. None of those guys ever talked to me. Their calling me names at the water fountain was not my idea of conversation. And of all of them to speak to me, why him? He was a whole year older than me and the school's best athlete. His bragging photos were all over our high school yearbook. And though the word was he was smarter than he let on, he always played the tough. His was a lumbering gait, side to side, arms held stiffly away from him as if he were ready to pick a fight. Him sitting so close made me want to jump away and run.

"What're you doing after you graduate?" An idiotic thing to say, but all I could come up with in my nervousness.

He sat upright, shrugged. Told me it was still a ways off. His father wouldn't have him working the booms, that was certain. No life, his dad warned him. "Wants me to get the education he never had. Promises to buy me a car if I pass everything."

"Sounds pretty cool."

"Yeah, right." He snorted. "We can't even afford a telephone. How's he going to buy me a goddamn car?"

Reaching forward with both hands, he balanced on his palms and, arm muscles tensing, inched closer. "I'd like to play basketball. You know, professional. I've scored highest in our division the past two years. But Coach says not to get my hopes up. It's rough, he says. Go broaden your horizons. Guess he's givin' me a hint. Like I'm not tall enough or somethin'.

"Ah," he said, surveying the marbled water, "maybe I'll try university, if I get the marks. At least it'll get me outta this dump."

"Yeah," I said. "Know what you mean." I followed his gaze and wished I were escaping on that deadhead to a new life in Vancouver.

Moments went by without us talking. Even so, he was constantly in motion, taking everything in, swatting at bugs, kicking up sprays of water. He pointed to an eagle, then cawed like a jay. I rested my chin on my hands, and when he wasn't watching, my eyes attempted glances along the log to the junction of his legs.

He returned his attention to me, gestured dramatically to the river. "Just look at the reflection of that cedar branch! The greens! The browns! The yellows in the water! And not a blue to be found!"

Put at ease by all his shenanigans, I laughed. At the same time, I sensed his eyes flickering along my backside and was excited. Fearful, too, that my spycraft would be detected, my carefully constructed exterior not a protection, but a trap.

A speedboat zipped along the river, heading toward the lake. He was shifting again, hoisting himself away from the log, swinging his legs, levering himself even closer. But this time as he settled, he lurched up and yelled, "Fuck! Fuckin' splinters!" He bent forward, fingers searching under his shorts for the source of the pain. They located the puncture, but when he seemed unable to find a purchase, he pulled the front of his briefs under his balls.

"Shit, it's a long one."

He inched up his leg and with the nails of his thumb and his forefinger manoeuvred the wooden sliver from his thigh. He presented it to me for inspection, then blew it in the river, as one might scatter the seed head of a dandelion for luck. Licking blood from his fingers, he splashed water on the cut and scrubbed a streak of red from his underwear.

Suddenly he jerked his head up, spotted me staring. "All right!" he barked, snapping the elastic band of his briefs back into place. "Show's over!" With an open hand, he slapped the water, sending icy sprays cascading down my face and back.

I gasped and scrambled to a sitting position. Shocked, embarrassed at having blown my cover to openly gape at him, anger shadowed my face and I splashed back. "Fuck you!"

For the first time we were seated eye to eye, and I struggled to maintain my gaze. The waves from the passing boat reached us. I softened when, beneath the water, his feet and shins floated against mine.

"Hey, it's okay. I was only teasin'." His extended hand tousled my hair as his lips spread into a grin.

My face flushed, something it still does all too easily.

"I do notice you around," he said. "Mainly noon hour, in the gym when the basketball team's practicin'. You're up in the bleachers readin', or sometimes with Jeffrey Hearn."

Jeffrey and me up in a dark corner, pretending to pay attention to the game, his leg slyly pressed into mine. His hand concealed under my heavy coat, exploring the knuckles of my spine. My heart pounding away as he did.

My voice rode up the scale as I struggled to suppress my alarm. "You know Jeffrey?"

"Not much." He gestured with his chin toward the lake. "His old man works up in camp too." He gave me a puzzled look. "So, you guys never play?"

It took a few moments to register what he was asking. "Play sports?"

"Yeah. You and Jeffrey are always hangin' out up in the stands. But I never see either of you play nothin'." His gaze raked over my body. "You got a long frame to put muscle on. You'd be good at basketball, I bet."

My mind rushed to years of clumsiness on the court, and I blushed. "I can't dribble. The bloody ball always gets away from me."

He tugged a wood chip from the log and flung it into the water. "It's just practice. I could teach you, if you want."

His straddling thighs kept drawing me in, and I had difficulty coming up with a response. At the same time, I was surprised and touched by his offer.

"I ... like to run," I said, finally finding a way in.

"Yeah, you got the legs for that. Long ..."

"And swimming. I like swimming ..."

"Yeah, I saw. Good form to build on."

His hand drifted up to rest on his shorts, fingers folded around the elastic band. Then, as if his knack for evaluating my sports potential extended to mind reading what I really desired, his other hand reached out to touch me.

Someone hollered from the far end of the boom at the mouth of the river. "Hey! We're takin' off. You comin'? You're gonna be late!"

He and I both started. Pushing himself off the log, he scrambled to his feet, sending the nearby timbers rocking. He gestured to the caller. "Wait! Wait up!" He bent his legs, plucked out the underwear's white cloth wedged in the cleft between his buttocks. "Guess I better join those ignoramuses. Gotta get to my shit job."

Even in my family's state of barely manageable poverty, my parents never required me to work. But I often saw him pumping gas at the station down the street from our house or in a white singlet, mowing lawns around town.

He glanced over at me. "You're burnin', by the way." Extending a finger, he poked my upper arm, leaving a ghostly trace. "Better cover up. You'll get sunstroke."

"Yeah," I said, excited, but also mortified by his mothering. "I will. Soon."

"And careful swimmin' for your colours, eh?" He gestured with his chin to the dark water mottled with sky. "Don't want them fishing out your body too."

I fought back that fear I'd experienced earlier, when swept away by the current. Though still slightly embarrassed over his concern, I was thrilled that someone as popular as him would take notice.

"Gotta run." He straightened, then lingered a moment, smiled. "Well, see you around."

"Sure, see you around," I said, keeping my voice flat, hoping to project casualness.

As he bounded off, I was rocked by the rolling motion of the log. I shut my eyes, wishing to blister into memory the image of his retreating, nearly naked body. When I opened them, he had almost reached the boom's edge. His feet barely touched the logs, and his outstretched arms fluttered at his sides, as if at any moment they would lift him to the sky.

After one last leap to the shore, he shimmied into a T-shirt, threaded his sturdy legs into jeans, and knelt to lace up his sneakers.

"Hey," I said, with a sudden rush of panic and affection. "What's your name?"

"Wade!" he shouted. "My name's Wade."

He rose to his feet and waved. Then, before fading through the salal onto the trail home, he unzipped his fly, sent an arc of yellow splashing into the water that lapped at his feet.

spawning grounds

WADE LET OUT a low whistle. "Holy shit, look at that!"

Below us, thousands of dead and dying salmon massed in the open river flats. Sun sparkled on water that threaded through sandbanks heaped with dull cinnamon-grey carcasses, their jaws agape as if grinning at some final joke.

Wade was studying their life cycle in Grade 12 science, which he had skipped so we could hitch the fifteen miles from Agassiz to these spawning grounds along the Harrison River. "Research." He smirked. "That's what we'll tell old man Northcott, if we get caught. I'm doin' research and you're my assistant."

We had hatched the plan to play hooky on the bus that morning, Wade bouncing alongside me. His hand resting lightly on my shoulder. We had no idea where we wanted to go, except to get away from the boredom of high school in that sleepy backwater, Agassiz.

"What about Chilliwack?" I said. As a child, I always loved going there. It is the biggest town at that end of the Valley, with a movie theatre, record shop, and even back then an Eaton's department store.

"Nah, fuckin' Fraser ferry takes forever. Someone might catch us and squeal." Wade flicked a well-aimed spitball three rows up, dinging Maureen Taylor on the back of her freshly coiffed poodle clip. "Can't wait till they finish that dang bridge. Then we can zoom over from Harrison in your old man's car and take girls to the drive-in." He beamed innocently as Maureen patted her hairdo and glared back at us.

The bus lurched into the school grounds, and Wade swayed into me. Just as it did every time we'd touched over the previous year and a half, this set off an electric jolt—an interplay of lust and affection.

I'd had very little experience with either of them as a sixteen-year-old. To fill that deep loneliness, I'd resorted—and not for the last time—to fantasy. I pictured myself a captive prince confined in a tall stone tower. There—with a ratty towel for a cape, a yardstick my sceptre, a baseball cap crown—I called out night and day for him to rescue me, though I did not know his name.

And, at last, he arrived. Or, at least, the semblance of him.

Wade's friendship—among its other joys—conferred a power I was completely unfamiliar with: popularity. As his sidekick, his social status as the school's top athlete was magically conferred on me. Nobody sniggered as I passed in the halls or called me Teddy Bear. When divvying up teams in PE, I was no longer habitually picked last. The two of us were invited to birthday parties or over to girls' houses at night to watch TV. I experienced a sense of optimism then and walked around in a poor mimicry of his confident gait.

"How about hitching north of the Fraser?" I said on the bus that day. "See how far rides'll take us?"

He hunched his shoulders and pursed his lips, which I considered a yes. So, after lunch hour, we slipped away from our afternoon classes and rendezvoused at the pool hall at the Bella Vista Hotel. Then we dashed across the Canadian Pacific tracks at the edge of town just before two sets of trains clattered by, one eastbound to the Rockies, the other west to Vancouver.

After a while, an elderly couple picked us up in a clunker that seemed nearly as old as they were. Rattling westward outside Agassiz, we sputtered past spent cornfields, their stubby stalks all ajumble. Past the milking sheds of tidy dairy farms. After climbing the forested rump of Mount Woodside, we crossed the bridge over the Harrison where the river bends to meet the Fraser—finally landing opposite Harrison Mills.

Except for some high cirrus near the western horizon, the day Wade and I played hooky was bright and clear, a relief from persistent October rains. Exhausted fish below us, still glistening and silver, thrashed about in shallow pools to lay their eggs while their decomposing brethren littered the river's bottom or lay heaped on its shores.

The stench was overpowering. To keep from retching, we covered our faces, bandit-like, with bandanas and eyeballed one another at close range. Even with his nose and mouth concealed, I could tell he was smiling. He wiggled his eyebrows, something he knew would get a chuckle out of me. Then, barrelling ahead, voice muffled by the polka-dotted cloth, he hollered over his shoulder, "Keep an eye out for bears!"

Leaving the highway behind, we scrambled through the bush down a steep embankment toward the river. A rock under my foot dislodged and I tumbled, crashing face down on a muddy shoal by the rushing water. Glowering at me, the empty socket of a picked-at carcass. I heard Wade's laughing put-down and, red faced, tried to scramble upright. Pain blasted from my left foot, and my leg collapsed me back onto the sandbar.

He rushed to where I was sprawled, helped me scramble to a sitting position. "What is it?"

"My foot," I groaned, my face contorting.

"Jesus, Teddy. It's not broken, is it?"

With my thumb, I gently probed the area below my ankle bone. "No, don't think so."

Bending down, he unlaced my sneaker, peeled off my sock, skimmed fingers over skin. "It's blazin' hot. Cold water'll keep the swelling down."

Heaving my arm over his shoulder, he snugged his hand around my waist, hoisted me up and urged me to hop toward the riffle on my good foot. With each movement, a pang shot from my ankle and ran along my leg. Wade guided me to shore, eased me down to a seat on a nearby rock. Kicking off his shoes, he slogged into the stream and lowered my foot into its freezing water.

He soaked his handkerchief, brushed mud from my cheek, all the while nagging me to hold still. Gently daubing my right brow, he told me there was blood above my eye. "Just surface, looks like. But you may wind up with a shiner." He peered closer, giving me his worried face.

At the beginning of our friendship, I'd distrusted his fussing over me like that. Thought it a set-up to some practical joke that would leave me sprawled on my backside or the brunt of more schoolyard teasing. By that day at the spawning grounds, though, I had grown comfortable with his looking after me, especially when no one was around. Just little things, like he was doing then, caused ease to spread throughout my body, the sensation of merging with moment and place.

The cold water numbing my foot, the throbbing decreased. I clambered onto the riverbank, balancing uneasily on one leg. Wade steadied me, then wheeled around and motioned for me to climb on. "Piggyback," he grunted. He hooked his arms under my thighs and we crouched forward. My forearms encircling his neck, my chin hammered the top of his head. I moved it aside, let it straddle his shoulder, my cheek nuzzling his ear.

Pressed against his body, as he trudged up the embankment, I awoke to the movement of the muscles in his back. His touch had never been as sustained or as whole bodied as that, causing the sensation of merging to return. I surrendered to it, my limbs dangling off his frame.

There was a spot in the tall grasses some distance from the riverbank, and by the time we reached it, we were both panting. I slid down his back until my good foot touched the ground, then he carefully released my legs. Pivoting around, he lowered me to a sitting position beside a log stranded there, escaped from a boom after a high-water spring runoff.

He knelt beside me. "All right?"

"Yeah, it's not so bad."

"Good," he said. He gathered up his shoes, laced them, then scrambled down the bank to leap across the water onto the sandbar. I watched him dart through the rocks, feinting suddenly side to side, as agile as when he danced the logs boomed on the river or charged down the basketball court at school. At times he stopped, bent down to examine something, poked around in the shallows with a stick, then sped off.

I relaxed against the log. Having grown used to the stink of rotting fish, I slipped the bandana off my face and let it drape from my neck. Near the opposite shore, a line of ghostly, grey timbers bristled from the water's surface. Pylons that once anchored booms of logs awaiting processing around the river bend at the ruined mill.

Rummaging through my knapsack, I retrieved the binoculars I often carried for birdwatching. I scolded myself for not packing the area's contour map that I kept pinned to my bedroom wall while focusing beyond the river. There, the western flank of Mount Woodside was swaddled in the reds and yellows of fall.

Through the lenses, the landscape compressed, flattened, like the pop-up books I'd loved as a young boy. Bulrushes, logs, rocks, trees, they were all two-dimensional as they receded in space.

I was suddenly placed in a memory of one of our hikes up Woodside. Wade and I had huffed up trails—overgrown with moss, sword fern, second-growth forest—that gradually disappeared. Then reappeared only to be lost again, till there was nothing but the sky and the upward contour of the terrain to guide us.

We bushwhacked through salal and devil's club, rounded moss-draped boulders, rotting cedar logs, and rust-red stumps teeming with huckleberry bushes. Caught our breath under huge cedars and firs, survivors of years of logging, wind, and fire.

At the summit, we came out onto a wide clear-cut; all askew on the ground were the remains of trees, stumps and branches yellowing in the fierce summer heat. Poking up through this debris, masses of purple-flowered fireweed were the only sign of life in that otherwise blasted landscape.

Below us spread the Fraser Valley, the electric-green hayfields and the dairy farms' well-trod plots, the roads and watersheds, even our school. To the north, we could just make out the Lillooet Range that brackets Harrison Lake. Eastward, appearing as if it were made with an Erector Set, was the Agassiz bridge being constructed over the glinting Fraser.

"Small," Wade had said. "Everything's so far away and small."

We'd remained there without talking for what must have been an hour. Birds flitted among the nearby trees as we tracked the deepening shadows across the valley on the snowfields clinging to the summit of Mount Cheam. That was the first I understood silence bound him to me.

At the school lunchroom, say, when his boisterousness waned and he broke from his friends, their mindless chatter about who was dating who or what chance our team had to win. His going to the steam tables for seconds always made me smile. I waited for it. It was a gambit he employed, a reason to come and sit by me until the bell. We sometimes caught up on homework or talked about books I was reading. But often we just sat and watched the light pour through the windows. I felt sorry for the other kids, who never saw this side of him.

I let the binoculars dangle from their strap and shifted my gaze from mountain to river. There was music stuck in my head suddenly, something classical Dad had played the previous night on our new hi-fi. Beethoven, I remember him saying.

Beside the rushing river, Wade shouted something I couldn't make out because of the blaring music in my head. To the accompaniment of a full orchestra, Wade leapt across rivulets—shadowing fish that wriggled through the shoals or hunching down to examine their carcasses. After pinching his nostrils and scowling, he righted himself, arched backward. Lifting his face to the sun, he bellowed a volley of body-shaking laughter, then bounded upriver around a bend and out of sight.

Turning my attention to the sky, I spied a sandhill crane. As the bird soared overhead, I tracked its lanky silhouette through my binoculars until I heard Wade gallop back.

"Scared a bear!" he said, gasping for breath. "Almost bumped right into him. We both jumped a mile. Jesus, do those things stink up close!"

"It didn't follow you, did it?" I cast a worried look behind him.

"Nah, we took off in opposite directions. They're way more interested now in salmon than humans."

Wade plunked down beside me. Under the stench of decomposing fish, a familiar scent—a trace of soap mingled with his sweat. Chest heaving, he was humming his own twisty version of "Rock Around the Clock."

I shushed him when I noticed, through the tall yellowing grass, a bald eagle circling some marshland next to the highway. I trailed the raptor with the glasses until it lit on one of the pylons near the opposite shore. Keeping the strap around my neck, I passed Wade the binoculars and visualized the encircled landscape as he located the bird. When he gestured toward the eagle, I softened into the sensation of the fine hairs of his boy-beard brushing against my cheek.

"Looks like a salmon in his claws. And he's tearin' it to pieces!" Wade scrutinized the bird as it devoured its meal. "Oops, there he goes."

With a few flaps of its broad wings, the eagle dropped the carcass and soared across the river toward a clear-cut that despoiled half a mountain range to the north.

I slipped a worn sketchbook from my pack and jotted down the sighting in my bird list. There were fewer baldies then, I had noted. And trumpeters. Something was getting them. Hunters, I speculated. Maybe logging. How naive and careless we all were back then.

Wade slumped against me, loosed the binoculars to drape from my neck. "You're gettin' real good at that," he said, spying my drawing of a bald eagle on the facing page. "So, what's its Latin name?"

"*Haliaeetus leucocephalus.*" I enunciated the words carefully, lovingly.

Wade grinned. "I can't believe you remember all that."

He stripped off his shirt. Scrubbing sweat from his body, he nosed his armpit and screwed up his face. The bedraggled handkerchief hung limply around his neck: blue dots against flushed, pale skin.

"Jesus, Wade," I said, motioning to the mottled purple bruises on his shoulder. "What the heck?"

"The old man," he said, face darkening, fingers gliding over the welts.

"Why'd he do that?"

Wade snorted. "Me skippin' school. Not helpin' enough around the farm." He smacked a deer fly on his arm, flicked off the blood-spattered remains. "Still thinks he can beat the shit out of me. One of these times I'll kill the sonofabitch."

Wade stared at the water riffling below, caressing again the bruises on his shoulder. "Why'd he buy that lousy farm anyway?"

My father was the affable groundskeeper and handyman at the local hot springs resort. A menial job, though a cushy one compared to Wade's dad, who for two decades had been a tree faller for a logging outfit up the lake. A year before, he'd quit, saying he was too old for scrambling over steep slopes lugging heavy equipment. He purchased a farm outside Agassiz, right against a mountain, north side. In shadow half the year round. No good for raising crops. A dumpy place and never enough money to fix it up.

Disappointment brought out the cruelty in his father, running off Wade's brothers—one to the RCMP, the other into the arms of a nursing assistant in Abbotsford. Wade's father, who had been so intent on his youngest son to focus on his education, then just wanted him to up his game around the farm.

I could never understand how this sour person won over Wade's sweet mother, no matter how many times Wade laid out the facts. How those two fell for each other in her hometown of Montreal, where Wade's dad was stationed prior to D-Day. How after the war, they eloped, since Wade's mother's French Canadian family was strictly Catholic and Wade's father was adamantly nothing at all. How the pious Monsieur Paquette disowned his daughter over the union and didn't speak a word to her after that.

"Makes me laugh," Wade said, "when he bitches about me being over at your house for dinner too much. 'Don't think we feed you good enough?'" Wade mimicked his father's high baritone. "I can tell he's itching for me to sass him, so he can teach me a lesson, but Mom rags at him to let me alone in Québécois. And for once the niaiseux, he can't say nothin'—the stupid fuck not botherin' to learn a lick of French."

Wade rose to his feet, shuffled over to some bushes to piss. I averted my gaze as he finished buttoning up. When he sat again, he reached across me, fished around in my shirt pocket, where he knew I kept smokes and matches.

"You're so lucky, you know," he said. "You live in town. Records. TV. Hell, you even have a phone."

He had the wrong idea about my family. We barely squeaked by with Dad's resort job and Mom part-time at the post office. I had been too embarrassed to confess that to Wade.

He rotated his head, spat, wrestled back into his shirt. "And your parents—they're so great. You can talk with them about everything."

"Not everything." My eyes darted from the vein bluing a line down the centre of his biceps to the spectacle of the dying fish.

Shaking two cigarettes from the crumpled pack, Wade fired them up and passed me one. "Sure squashed the shit out of these," he said. Reclining against the log, his arm settled easily across my shoulders.

Another moment of quiet descended upon us, contented as we were to watch the river parade along its broad curve toward the Fraser. While we smoked, I shot glances at his profile. His forehead and nose were at the same angle; you could ski down them without hitting a bump. It reminded me of those other pictures in the encyclopedia, the ones I would pore over in the school library after I made sure no one was around. Ogling those statues of handsome, naked Greek gods. And Wade, he looked just like them: his gorgeous face, his muscles so defined and taut, as if they, too, were chiselled from a block of marble. As he aged, he developed even more compelling masculine attributes—a black moustache, a thicker, more heavily muscled body, and a sharply angular jaw—but what really stirred me back then was the classical angle of his nose and brow.

It is nearly unfathomable how shameful those feelings were, now having lived openly for so long, and having had these desires since earliest memory. There's this one—when I must have been only four or five. A friend from down the street and I were leafing through a copy of *Life* magazine. We came across a photo of soldiers lined up for inoculations before they were shipped out to Korea. At the sight of their shirtless bodies, little sparks of pleasure tripped up my spine. My friend continued paging through the magazine, but I kept flipping back to see if the soldiers had removed their pants.

It occurs to me some of the men in that picture must have been killed in the war. All my life I had witnessed the ritual of salmon dying, but it was just something that happened each year, like the beginning of school or changes in the weather. Though I am now all too familiar with death, my experience of it at that time was relegated to the May afternoon when I thought I might drown in that river, and an occasion when I was seven. When Mom had moved her brother Bill into the back of our little house.

Even then, my parents were old—having waited so long in life to marry—but Bill was older still, an infantryman in World War I. Apparently, he'd begged Mom to spring him from the veterans' hospital in Vancouver, where he had been convalescing from another breakdown.

I was made to sit opposite him for meals at the dining table. Watching him shovel food into his gob, his face bristly, his skin a sickly yellow, I found him repulsive and was generally chilly toward him. One night, though, my mother invited our old codger neighbour over for supper, probably thinking my uncle could use a friend. Our guest took my usual place at the table, so I sat next to Bill. When I couldn't gawp at him, my uncle seemed surprisingly agreeable, funny even, and I enjoyed the friendly talk throughout the meal.

Afterward, while I worked on my school assignments in the kitchen, the two old men huddled on the chesterfield in the living room, speaking softly. From what I could make out, they were comparing notes on what had happened to them during the war.

The excitement, or maybe the awfulness of remembering, were too much for Uncle Bill's ticker. In his room the next morning, I observed Mom hold a mirror under his nose to find he was no longer breathing.

On the shoals below Wade and me, troops of shrieking seagulls tussled over scraps of rotting, dull-grey flesh. I drew on the cigarette, cleared my throat and motioned to the salmon snaking noisily through the shallows. "What does Northcott say? Why the heck do they do this? It's crazy, coming all the way here from the Pacific."

Wade squinted at me, his hand shielding his eyes from the low autumn sun. "To screw, or whatever. Lay their eggs and croak." He pulled on his cigarette, pursed his lips and discharged a wispy circle. "I wonder if they realize they've saved the best for last?"

"Come on, Wade. They don't have that kind of awareness." I flicked away an ant scuttling across my bare, bruised foot. "With them, it's more like instinct."

"Instincts." A wolfish grin blooming across his face, he removed his arm from my shoulders. "I'd like to follow my instincts with Maureen Taylor. Wouldn't you with Joanne?"

I found that idea laughable. I had known my schoolmate Joanne for a year and considered her more of a pal than anything else.

Directly below us, an exhausted salmon flailed about in a too-shallow pool, its scales flashing bright red. A couple of ravens were positioned to one side, waiting.

"Tell you what," Wade said, dropping his cigarette and crushing it with the heel of his shoe. "If they knew they were going to die, they wouldn't follow their fucking instincts."

I hobbled away from the smell and racket. Back by the side of the highway, Wade and I waited for some car to come along, stop, and drive us home. Now that we were in the long shadows of hemlock, away from the sun-warmed river flats, the temperature was dropping steadily to freezing. A biting breeze picked up, and I hunched my shoulders and zipped my thin windbreaker up to my neck.

Wade cradled my chin in his fingertips, torqued my head to the side to examine my face. "Shit, look at that black eye! It's a beaut, all right. What're you gonna tell your old man?"

I planned to invent a story about standing up to a bully at recess—something improbable to please him. What really worried me was how we would fake our notes explaining our absence from school, how we would forge our parents' signatures. There would be hell to pay if Wade didn't get his just right.

No passing cars were to be found, but finally a rumbling approached from around the bend. A brand new '57 Chevy barrelled into view, bright red and shiny. We stuck out our thumbs. It zoomed by, then veered onto the side of the road and skidded to a stop. Streaming out one of the car's partially open windows, the blocky piano chords of Jerry Lee Lewis's "Great Balls of Fire."

With me limping behind, Wade sprinted ahead, shouting, "Bel Air! And lookit the whitewalls!"

There was only the driver inside—a middle-aged businessman, his tie askew, the top shirt button undone. He cranked Jerry Lee Lewis off, then grabbed the rumpled suit coat on the plastic two-toned banquette and flung it in the back.

Since it was my turn up front, I called shotgun and slipped in next to the man. Wade had hardly wedged himself in the back when the driver floored it, tires spitting gravel onto the shoulder before they squealed onto the blacktop.

"Where you boys going?" The man gave us a broad smile that contrasted with his bloodshot eyes, his slumped demeanour. His words were slurred slightly, and it smelled like he had been at the hard stuff.

I was getting anxious and angled around to see if Wade was feeling the same. But he must have worn himself out earlier, because his head was bobbing forward, then jerking upright, his mouth wide open.

Looking Wade over in the rear-view, the driver stiffened, gripped the steering wheel hard. White peaks under the skin at his knuckles, a gold wedding band nestled among them.

"You from around here?" the man asked, practically staring holes into the side of my face. The car swerved onto the shoulder, stones noisily battering its undercarriage.

Wide-eyed, I gawked straight ahead at the strobing white line.

The man downshifted as we began the long descent on the south slope of Mount Woodside. The view of the brightly lit plots of farmland below was darkly tunnelled by the overarching trees.

"What happened to your face?"

With a fingertip I patted the tender spot under my right eye. "I fell when we were messing around at the river."

"Looks like you got into a fight. You like to fight, don't you? Bet you're a tough guy."

I sensed him ogling me again, a warmth on that side of my body. I was unsettled when I turned to look at him; his eyes seemed so sad. I jolted with desire as well when I noticed, finally, how handsome he was.

I gaped in the back. "Wade?" I called out, but he was still fast asleep.

All of a sudden, the man's hand was on my knee, and it started creeping up my thigh. I jerked around, glared straight ahead, immobilized by the heat of his touch.

He grunted, almost inaudibly. I gawked down at his fingers stroking my stiffening cock through my jeans. My head fell against the seatback. A shimmering sensation prickled up my spine. I gasped as fingers fumbled with the buttons of my fly.

Then there was the squeal of wheels skidding on asphalt and Wade screaming, "Fuckin' pull over and let us out!" He was leaning in, punching the back of the man's head. We nearly plowed into a fully loaded logging truck before the driver regained control of the car, and it swerved to a stop.

His face had turned a deep crimson. His shoulders bowed, he stared out the side window as Wade and I scrambled from the car. When the man turned to me, his eyes were pleading.

Wade wrenched the door shut and the driver peeled away, but not before Wade got a good kick in. Denting the car's side panel, he bellowed, "Fuckin' cocksucker! Get the fuck outta here!"

I stalked off down the road a few paces, my breath shallow, my hands cupped at my waist. Everything I'd feared was coming true, my carefully crafted deceptions exposed. My thoughts raced ahead, calling up a succession of quick, barely perceived excuses. Pathetic lies, all.

Wade was kicking rocks and swearing, telling me that it had happened before and the next time he was going to kill any fucking queer that laid a hand on him. He spun around and, veins bulging on the side of his neck, he shouted, "Why the hell did you let him touch you like that?"

He screwed up his face, forehead furrowed, jaw slack, his glistening eyes half shut. There was a faint trembling in his lower lip. This was all so out of character, I was suddenly frightened. From the way he balled up his fists, I feared, too, he was going to swing at me. Then his expression morphed into something far worse; the look of confusion he then gave me was shot through with distrust.

I cowered backward, started to speak, but he shouted, "Shut up!" He threw a handful of rocks in the direction of the Bel Air, tiny now, banking through the sunlit fields at the bottom of the hill.

We didn't try for another ride but instead clambered down an embankment thick with salal, the sheen on their leaves dulled by highway dust. I clutched tree limbs to slow my progress, attempting to keep my weight off the injured foot.

Halfway down the slope, Wade slipped, cussing as he tumbled to the bottom. When I reached him, he had picked himself up and was brushing dirt and leaves from his shirt and jeans.

I tapped him on the shoulder. "You okay?"

He shoved me away, hard, so I stumbled backward, falling, my sprained ankle shrieking with pain. He glowered down at me, hands and jaw clenched. Scrambling to my feet, I shrank away, my anger thinly masking an unsettling new insecurity with Wade. Through my clenched teeth I muttered, "Fuck you too."

I shambled through a stand of old fir and cedar toward the marsh I had spotted earlier. Near the water's edge I came upon a log, soft with decay and moss, an earthy smell from its ranks of gloppy fungus. Some of the wood fragmented in my hands into rich russet cedar chunks. I took a seat, dug out my binoculars and, to calm myself, scanned the scene before me. Chickadees and red-winged blackbirds flitted among the bulrushes—their battered tan stalks mirrored at all angles on the water.

I kept an ear cocked for any sound of Wade but heard none. Sensations from the man's touch resurfaced, and it was an excitement I didn't want to stop. I could almost feel his hand caressing my thigh. My breath quickened as I imagined my fly bursting open, his fingers stealing into my shorts.

Muffled by the carpet-like moss, Wade's footsteps came to a halt directly behind me, causing the hair to prickle on the back of my neck. I resumed peering through the binoculars, tracked the seed heads of rushes drifting like cotton in the breeze. He perched on the log an arm's length away, loitered there, as if he were sharing a park bench with a stranger. A new kind of silence descended on us. Unsettling. Nervous.

I struggled to find words to fill this breach between us, but none came. Retrieving the pack of cigarettes from my shirt pocket, I shook out a crumpled smoke. As he plucked it from my hand, our fingers brushed lightly. I tensed and struck a match into flame.

After a while, he started noticing the birds, so I handed him the binoculars, and he rambled along the bank, smoking and observing things, which appeared to take his mind off what had happened. He trained the glasses on a blue heron wading through the marsh, its attention on something just below the surface. As it stalked through the cattails, Wade trod quietly, his slow, wide steps mimicking the heron's elegant gait.

Wade lost his balance on the spongy moss in a jerky dance of flailing arms and legs and curses. Startled, the heron took flight in its own whir of flapping limbs. We traced its laborious ascent until it coasted over the treetops.

Inexplicably, Wade stormed off, arms held above his head, bushwhacking through a thicket of waist-high salal to disappear into a stand of hemlock.

I closed my eyes, greedily recalling the heat of the man's touch. The image was marred by another. My schoolmate Jeffrey Hearn feeling me up in the bleachers while Wade and his teammates scuttled around the basketball court. My fear and excitement as—hidden under my winter coat—the boy's fingers traced the ridge of my spine.

Then I saw him on the school bus one afternoon, distraught and crying. Having no protector, as I had, he'd been bullied on the playing field earlier by a gang of older boys. Stuck with the "fruit" label, he never returned to school after that. He and his family moved. All the way to Kamloops, somebody once said. I dislodged the memory, opened my eyes, staunched the rising in my throat.

Noting the marsh freezing over, I trudged to its edge and examined the ice—all angular, shooting out from the bank and joining up. A tracery of crystal that had begun its spread through the wetland.

A twig crunched behind me. I jumped. Spun around.

Wade was cradling a young mallard to his chest. He knelt, restrained the bird against the ground, the binoculars that dangled from his neck swaying below him.

"Look," he said, "somethin's got it. Wing's broken." The bird struggled in his grip, and he whispered, "It's okay, it's okay."

He stroked its bobbing head for a moment, then snapped its neck. From his crouched position, he scowled at me. "What? You never seen somethin' put out of its misery?"

He positioned the quivering body under a bush, brushed his hands on his thighs. He rose to his feet, his silhouette reflected on the marsh's surface. "Maybe that eagle will find it, have a good meal."

A movement caught his eye—the returning blue heron descending through the bulrushes. He monitored its progress in the binoculars. Then, sidestepping, he focused on my face to glower at me through the lenses.

Unable to bear this, I diverted my gaze to the marsh, the skim of ice expanding across its water. At first an almost invisible barrier, it was then a milky haze masking the roots and algae-slicked branches. The teeming life and decomposition below. Slowly, it was erasing our reflections.

drive-in

I WAS CRUSHED inside my father's '58 Studebaker at the Chilliwack Drive-In—trapped between the door, the steering wheel, and Joanne—the air stifling, the windows fogged, the heater working overtime against the chill of an April evening. In the back seat, Wade was necking enthusiastically with Maureen Taylor, judging by the sounds of smacking lips, sighs, and the rustling of clothes.

Joanne loomed over me, her breath heaving, her cardigan draped open to disclose her busty blouse front. She wrestled with the top button of my shirt, as inches away, her upturned lips closed in on mine. To discourage this sudden onslaught, I reached across her with my handkerchief to clear the windshield, then attempted to redirect her attention to the movie.

On the big screen, the cowboy hero and his sidekick were galloping their pinto ponies around the badlands of the American Southwest. The arid buttes and canyons, bristly with cactus, so unlike the Fraser Valley, where our cedar- and moss-covered mountains are shrouded in mist and rain most of the year.

When the inevitable happened and Joanne clamped her lips over mine, my tongue cowered in the back of my mouth. I turned my head aside to gulp for air each time her tongue stormed the gate to probe for mine. After a couple of these manoeuvres, she positioned my hand on her left breast. Sensing the bra shifting on the yielding flesh, my fingers stiffened.

Going that far was not what I had in mind.

It was opening weekend at the drive-in, and we'd reached Chilliwack in record time. Thanks to the new bridge, no more dawdling ferries crossing the Fraser, their shutdowns at night cooping us up on the Agassiz side. But what really got us to the show so quickly was Wade egging me on to GUN IT!

I'd concocted this double date in order to be close to him again. With the fallout over the hitchhiking incident the previous autumn—and with Maureen then in the picture—he maintained his distance, preferring to keep company with me in groups of other kids. And our rare alone times were never quiet, the space between us filled with his fast talk about cars and girls. Worse yet, he no longer referred to me as his best friend.

As for Joanne, her long blond hair framed a handsome, freckled face that centred on a pert, upturned nose. She was popular, class president, though I didn't have the option of holding that against her, since with Wade's neglect, she was practically my only friend.

After her family relocated to Harrison nearly two years before, most afternoons found us at the A&W, gabbing over burgers and shakes about movies, the stacks of books we both had on the go. Weekends, we'd sail our end of the lake in her father's boat—scarcely used since, as our town's harried resort manager, he had little opportunity to enjoy it.

Despite never considering Joanne and me to be dating, I didn't discourage the idea among the other kids. Believing myself to be behind enemy lines, I regarded my association with her—enjoyable though it was—as insurance against any rumours Wade might let slip about me.

So, after homeroom, I invited her on the double date. She bear-hugged me in reply, twirled us down the hall, and—with an audience of several others—foisted on me a gushy kiss. I realized then I should've paid more attention to the signs.

In the car, she was in full sumo wrestler mode, pinning me against the door and, as in most boys' dreams, smothering me with her breasts. In a kind of dissociative state, I imagined the door flying open, the two of us tumbling out, sprawled on the ground with everyone jeering and pointing. At this image, I burst out laughing in the middle of a particularly hefty kiss.

Joanne's eyes flashed open. "What's so funny, Teddy?"

"I don't know. Nothing?" I garbled the words—trying to prevent my voice from pitching upward—which caused me to laugh even harder. She had really laid her perfume on that night, I suppose trying to sharpen her appeal. It irritated my nose, and I had been holding back a sneeze. Suddenly I let it fly.

"Yuck! What's got into you?" She pushed off my chest with one hand, the other rushing to cover the mucus on her cheek.

"Sorry!" I stammered, strangling back even more laughter, all the while attempting to wipe her cheek with my handkerchief. She batted my hand away, grabbed the limp white cloth, and dabbed it at her face.

My own face burned with embarrassment. And in the stuffy heat inside the car, the sweat dripping from my forehead stung my eyes. A laugh track like those played in radio comedy shows niggled at the back of my mind, which started me up again. Great horse laughs delivered to her beautiful, scowling face.

"Jeez, Teddy. You can be such a bloody jerk!" She flung the handkerchief in my face.

"Hey, what's goin' on up there?"

I folded my legs back under the steering wheel and bolted to a sitting position. I glanced in the rear-view mirror straight into Wade's eyes. They took me aback, causing a hitch in my breath. He scrutinized me, as always—ever since I allowed the man in the Bel Air to grope me—with some kind of question or accusation.

"Just laughing," I said, as if it were the most natural thing one might do in that situation.

"Well, keep it down. We can't hear the movie."

Oh sure, I bet you can't, I thought, spying him again in the rear-view, his shirt unbuttoned practically to his navel, and Maureen and her newly blond poodle clip nowhere in sight. My eyes darted to Joanne slumped against the far door, fidgeting with the handle. She appeared ready to kill. Or cry. I swivelled around, kicked my door open, and scrambled out.

"Hey, where you goin'?" Wade said.

I blurted the first thing that popped into my head. "Snack bar. Anybody want anything? Popcorn? Coke?"

Joanne spit a command to the windshield. "7 Up, burger, and chips. With vinegar."

Wade swigged from one of the beers that he had cached under the back seat. "Wait! Wait up. Need to piss bad."

Halfway out the door, he was buttoning his shirt and adjusting his jeans—hand-me-downs, I knew, from one of his brothers. With Joanne peeved and unoccupied, I was certain he didn't want to be cramped in the car any more than I did.

"I'll get us burgers." Wade winked at Maureen as he wrestled back into the letter jacket he'd been awarded the previous year for varsity basketball.

Maureen had plump cheeks, a prominent nose, and a round face that bore a habitual look of surprise. She seemed startled by Wade's abrupt exit. Embarrassed too over my having witnessed her lacy bra bordered by an undone blouse, her rumpled plaid skirt hiked past her knees.

Wade picked a comb from his jeans pocket and reconfigured his straight black hair into its greasy ducktail. With a bandana, he swiped dust from the snakeskin boots he'd bought when he and I browsed the Chilliwack thrift stores. After easing his door shut, he faced me. My eyes flickered away, not wanting to be caught ogling the erection that I assumed strained against his tight-fitting jeans.

We threaded through lines of darkened cars. To our right, the last of the light silhouetted the Coast Mountains as they gently receded toward Vancouver and the Pacific, eighty miles to the west.

Wade cradled his hand around my neck, something I yearned for that he then rarely did. With this embrace, my shoulders tracked downward, my jaw slackened. He gestured with his head back to the girls. "What was that all about, you laughing at Joanne?"

I tensed again, caught the scent of Maureen's cologne on his fingers, and shrugged off his hand. "I wasn't laughing at her. I just imagined how funny it would be if the car door flew open and we spilled out, and everybody was laughing at *us*."

"What the hell's so funny about that?"

"I don't know. What the hell's funny about anything?"

Clenching my forearm, he yanked me to a stop. On the screen, a parade of covered wagons struggled up a dusty draw. The cowboy hero and his loyal sidekick maintained a wary eye ahead at the canyon the wagon train was compelled to pass through. With its stock characters and overacting, this movie would certainly not have been one Joanne and I ever discussed. Her tastes ran to musicals, mine to the psychological theatricality of Alfred Hitchcock.

Wade dug his fingers into my arm. His grasp smarted, but I wouldn't pull away. "She sure didn't think it was funny," he said. "Joanne's a looker, Teddy. In case you haven't noticed. Most guys are too chickenshit to ask her out, yet there she was, all over you!"

"Guess I'm not into it as much as you are with Maureen. Looked like you were about to bust your buttons."

He chuckled at that. A moment later, though, his smile withered and was replaced by the confused scowl he normally levelled at me.

"She obviously likes you."

"And I like her."

"So, what's the problem?"

When I remained silent, he released me, shaking his head. "You can be so fucking oblivious."

I rubbed the aching sensation in my forearm, stifled another laugh. How bloody oblivious *he* was to my struggle to stop my hands from tracking my urges.

Like the previous summer, him and me guzzling bootleg booze, jammed next to each other in the bed of a pickup, bombing up logging roads at dusk with a gang of other teenagers. Braking, accelerating at switchbacks. At every bump of the road, jolting when I crashed into him.

Or that night, when all of us were on a remote mountaintop above Harrison Lake, whooping and hollering around a campfire, staggering drunk. As I was retching, stumbling toward a cliff, it was Wade who grabbed me—Wade with the freedom to link his arms under mine, to press in with his body. Keeping me upright and steady, keeping me safe. How oblivious was he then to my not daring to turn and embrace him.

On the screen behind him, the hero's handsome profile. Straight dark hair just like Wade's spilled out from under the cowboy's white broad-brimmed hat. The camera pulled back to reveal him slugging some grizzled old coot, who crumpled onto a poker table, cards and chips flying. Pistols drawn, his lanky sidekick warned off anyone foolish enough to come to the cheater's defence. And crouching nearby, just off the stagecoach from Laramie, a beautiful woman decked out in a high-collared chequered dress. Her eyes wide, one gloved hand concealing her mouth.

When Wade fetched the smokes and matches I had stashed in my shirt pocket, I jolted.

"Jesus, Teddy. Why you so jumpy?" His right brow lifted and his eyes narrowed as he passed me a cigarette. With a scrape of his thumbnail, he ignited a wooden match. The phosphorous burst illuminated hands callused from heavy work on his family's farm. Inching close, he cupped his fingers around the flame to shelter it from a breeze.

I yearned to enclose those hands in mine. But I had witnessed them punching out guys bigger and older than me, including his father. Watched them string up a deer, slit its stomach so its organs tumbled out.

"You gonna take a drag or just stare at it?" He thrust the flame toward me, then lit his own cigarette. He flicked out the match and tossed it onto the gravelled lot. Pointing in the direction of the washrooms, he said he was off to take a leak.

I told him I would meet him at the snack bar. I needed to relieve myself as well but would find an excuse later. I would have been too tense, Wade beside me at a urinal, relaxed and pissing like a thoroughbred, with me picturing Niagara Falls to persuade nature to take its course.

Something similar occurred after gym class in the school showers—only the opposite. Wade across from me, humming "Jailhouse Rock" or another song, while I trained my mind on icebergs, the *Titanic* sinking, the threat of an imminent watery death. Still, the inevitable happened. When I watched him soaping up his muscled frame, I was forced to make a fast getaway, grabbing the nearest towel for cover, fearing someone had caught sight of the reason why.

When I reached the snack bar, I barked out our orders. The aroma of frying onions permeated the air. Since there was no place to sit, I leaned against a wall, coasted down the stubbly concrete to the dirt lot, and hugged my knees to my chest. Beyond the big screen, Chilliwack's squat warehouses, the glow on the western horizon—Vancouver smudging the undersides of clouds.

I scolded myself for trying to renew my friendship with Wade. But it was the special understanding I'd long fantasized. Though sexless—second-hand, even, with that pathetic double date—the thought of losing it was unbearable.

Smoke scorched my lungs as I took another pull from my cigarette. I fingered the sore spot on my forearm that lingered from Wade's hard grasp. The scent of Joanne's perfume fouled my shirt. From a radio propped on the counter blared a steady beat—Jerry Lee Lewis hammering on a raspy piano the opening chords of "Great Balls of Fire."

Intruding on my thoughts, the stench of rotting salmon. That previous fall afternoon by the river. The Bel Air, the sunlight glinting off its bright-red finish. I bowed my head, my brow resting on my arms, my eyes shut. I smelled the liquor on the driver's breath. Felt his hand run along my thigh. The electric sensation shooting to my groin as he fumbled with the buttons of my fly. I witnessed Wade punching the man. The car peeling off. Wade on the side of the road, giving me that look of confusion, shouting, "Why the hell did you let him touch you like that?"

The song on the radio changed, "Hound Dog" filtering through the snack bar window. I lifted my head, opened my eyes to see Wade up on the balls of his boots, swivelling on Elvis hips, while he strummed the air and mouthed the lyrics into an imaginary microphone.

"What're you doin' down there? Lost your only friend?" He delivered my foot a quick kick. "You put in our order?"

I nodded.

"Then he's sure takin' his time. Hey, you!" He slapped the counter. "Can't you speed it up? I'm starving!"

Wade whirled around on his boot heels, swooping arms—fingers outspread—arcing to a halt at his right side. Like always, I took such pleasure in watching his moves and the way the leather jacket hugged his broad shoulders and tapered to his hips.

My gaze followed his to the screen. Against a blazing red sunset, the wagon train was on the move again, winding through sagebrush and giant saguaro, the landscape in the distance barbed with craggy spires.

"It's so different down there." His voice softened. "The Southwest. Blue skies every day! Not like rainy old here."

He hunched down the wall, squatting beside me. "I want to see it for real!" He crept closer, our knees almost touching. "We could get away from this shithole. You and me," he said, excitement animating his voice. "Don't care what my old man says. I can make real money logging up the lake this year. Buy some cheap wheels. We could drive down there next spring, soon as you're done with high school. Like in that beatnik book you and Joanne have been going on about—all the adventures those guys had road-tripping to San Fran! Only with us, we'd be banging across the line, down to Salt Lake, Vegas, the Grand Canyon. And then—boom! The Arizona badlands! It'd be so cool! What do you say?"

After taking one last drag from my smoke, then tossing it away, I gaped at him in disbelief. It was as if in his passion for this plan he had forgotten the incident the previous year, his pulling away ever since. I was desperate to escape our backwater as much as Wade, but not farther into the wilderness. Lately, Joanne and I had been scheming about heading to Vancouver after we graduated. Likely university, if I pulled up my grades.

As it always did, though, Wade's enthusiasm carried me away. For a minute, I succumbed again to fantasy, the two of us tearing through the sagebrush and cactus, he that handsome, dark-haired hero up on the screen, me the lanky twin of his doting sidekick. I observed us from high above, as if in a crane shot, pulling over for the night in the middle of nowhere: a campfire, sleeping bags rolled out, zipped in tandem ... But then bubbles swarmed through the image, and it was as if the film had flared and blackened, isolating me in a frame of blinding white.

When I offered no response, Wade fixed his eyes on me and scowled, his expression—invariably so assured and determined—clouded with disappointment. It always took me aback when I found, like this, that I was capable of hurting his feelings.

He leapt to his feet, hammered the counter bell twice. "Guy must be sleepin' at the wheel—there's no one else here."

A man finally appeared in the opening, his belly fairly bursting a sweat-stained and splattered chef coat. Scowling at Wade, he extended an arm and presented two oily paper sacks. Wade snatched them from his hand, tossed a ten-spot on the counter.

Reaching down, he yanked me up—nearly jerking my arm from its socket—then proceeded to wolf down his burger before we had rounded the corner, back of the snack bar.

There, in its shadow, he belched, craned his head up to lose himself again in the Technicolor landscape on the screen, the giant figures.

The muffled drone of actors reciting their lines, white noise from the rows of cars in front of us. Windows fogged, and girls and boys huddled close, necking. That scene appeared as alien to me as what was happening in the movie—the cowboy hero, smoke swirling from the end of his pistol, held open his arms for the woman in the chequered dress to rush into. To conceal my discomfort, I laughed.

Wade's gaze wrenched from the screen to me, his jaw clenched, feet kicking at the gravel. "It's all so funny to you." The anger in his voice contained a new hostile edge. "You think I'll never get out of this place. That it's some wild goose chase, me wanting to see those places up there and have adventures. Not like you—cooped up in a university classroom for years, everything all planned out."

My life all planned out? I struggled not to burst out laughing at that, understanding it would anger Wade even more. My only plan then was to find refuge in the anonymity of Vancouver—far from the gnawing isolation I experienced in Harrison.

"I was laughing at the movie. Not you," I said. "Your idea to go down south, it's not a wild goose chase. That's not what I think."

Wade yanked the pack from my shirt pocket and tapped out another smoke. He fired it up but didn't offer me one. Stepping directly in front of me, he took a long drag, exhaled. The smoke gusted across my face, and I recoiled against the wall.

"It's just … it's not a good idea for me right now," I stammered. "It's not what I want."

"Then what *do* you want? Tell me. I've been wonderin'."

Immobilized, pinned like an insect on a Styrofoam block, I faced away from his glare. Again I didn't reply.

Music swelled, tinny sounding from the car speakers. Up on the screen, the cowboy hero embraced the beautiful woman, his hands resting on her shoulders, nestled against the collar of her chequered dress. She snugged one arm around his waist as her fingertips caressed his cheek.

For a moment, the film cut to a figure in the shadow. The hero's lanky sidekick blinking back a tear. Then the hero again, gazing with love and adoration into the woman's eyes. The camera pushed in for a tight shot on the kiss.

Wade tracked my gaze in time to see this. When he turned back to me, he had a crooked smile on his lips. "That's what we should be doing." Dropping his smoke, he motioned toward the bright figures. "We should be kissing. And making out. Like up there."

I glanced from Wade to the screen, then back, and would have warded off my discomfort with another laugh, were it not for the sensation I had of falling almost imperceptibly forward, drawn to the beautiful double arcs of his lips. "*We*?" I heard myself say, my voice barely audible. "What do you mean, *we*?"

His brows contracted, and that grim questioning expression raked across his face. "That we should be back at the car, kissing. The girls. What else would I mean, Teddy?" Now he was the one laughing, spittle flying all over.

Revolted by the surge of his stale beer breath, the tobacco stink seeping off his clothes, I shoved him away, wiped his spit from my face with the back of my hand. "Wade, what's the matter with you?"

"What the fuck's the matter with *me*?"

Suddenly fearful at having nearly exposed myself, a patch of sweat seeped through my thin shirt at my armpits. I shivered in the chill of this early spring night. The action on the screen grabbed my attention, causing Wade to twist around and watch.

Alone now, the sidekick rode under a starless sky, his horse lumbering down a deserted street past a frontier town's false storefronts, their windows shuttered and dark. Two desiccated tumbleweeds raced past him as the camera dollied in for a close-up. Filling the frame, the sidekick's stricken face—tears in his narrowed, downcast eyes, his mouth contorted in a sickly grin.

That was me up there. Cast off.

My love lost to some nice girl with puffy cheeks and a fake blond coif.

A desperate welling from my gut. Pinpricks swarmed about my eyes. My anguish gushed out in heaving sobs, hot gobs of snot pooling on my upper lip.

Wade angled around to examine the pitiful spectacle of me, then looked to the screen once more to take in the despair of my solitary twin. Returning to my snivelling, he scowled his disapproval. Only his expression was stripped of its confusion.

His lips curled into a grimace.

A grimace that said, *Now I know what you want.*

Through the rear window of the Studebaker, I noticed Joanne had switched to the back seat with Maureen. They were giggling and horsing around, fingers snapping to the music, having a grand time. The movie's soundtrack was turned off, the radio on. Through the car windows, dull waves of static, the Del-Vikings crooning "Come Go with Me," probably from a Vancouver station. Or maybe Seattle or Bellingham, across the line.

The girls had reapplied their lipstick, and Maureen was holding a tiny compact in front of her face, primping her blond hairdo. Joanne shifted in her seat to take in Maureen, puckered her lips while making smooching sounds, until they burst out laughing again.

I rapped lightly on the glass. Not daring to show Joanne my reddened, swollen face, I averted my gaze toward the screen and held out the greasy bag. "Hamburger, chips, and a 7, coming Up."

I delivered the line to the rows of cars in front of me, my voice sounding hollow, the banter a failure to mask the turmoil I felt at having been found out at last. But beneath that torment, there must have been some slight relief at finally having been freed of the difficulty of loving Wade.

Joanne rolled down the window, plucked my offering from my hand. When I heard Wade's footsteps scuffling through the gravel, I swung open the driver's side door and quickly shut it behind me, sealing myself at the wheel.

Wade jerked open the rear door, and Joanne waved him away with the back of her hand. "We're fine here. You can sit up front with Teddy."

With Wade glaring, Maureen leaned forward and snickered, blew him a kiss. Thrusting the door shut, Wade spun on his heels, rounded the hood of the car to slump down on the banquette beside me. He stretched his left arm along the seatback, then yanked it off and shrank away.

I silenced the radio and turned up the volume on the speaker clipped to my window. "What's happened in the movie?" I said, as if I hadn't tracked nearly every moment.

Joanne rolled her eyes and turned to Maureen. "It's dumb," she and Maureen said at the same time, as though they had rehearsed the line.

"Stupid guys playing at being cowboys. So boring." Joanne smirked. "We've seen it all before. Bang, bang. Big deal."

Maureen jumped in. "Yeah, all those cowboys busting each other's chops! Ka-pow!" Her small fists punched the air.

"And what are they fighting over?" Joanne held up both hands, making as if she were conducting an orchestra.

"The girls!" they shrieked in unison and doubled over in another round of laughter.

I shifted in my seat and peered at Wade. He was slouched against his door, scowling out the side window. I checked myself in the rear-view. The eyes in my wide, still-boyish face were puffy and red. When I snapped the mirror back into place, I was startled by Joanne, staring right at me, giving me a worried expression.

From the metal speaker, the music swelled.

We were frozen there in silence, watching the credits roll. "THE END" finally floated off the screen. My mouth opened to laugh, but nothing would come out.

smouldering

IT HAD BEEN a summer of forest fires. They had been smouldering and flaring for weeks on a mountain up the lake, for miles the air heavy with smoke. Chunks of charred timber drifted in the water, and at night from the shorefront of Harrison you could see light trails on the dark mountainside. Everyone was on the lookout for falling cinders.

One Sunday afternoon—the middle of August, over a year after that awful night at the Chilliwack Drive-In—Joanne and I fled the beach gear–laden tourists thronging our village and set out in my father's Studebaker for a former logging camp—now a park across the lake.

The winding, newly built road was generally little used but bustling that day. A logging truck—its bunks stacked high with raw timber—roared by in the opposite direction, nearly forcing me into the cliff that walled our side of the narrow road. Startling us moments later, racing past were two pickups laden with firefighters, part of the growing numbers bound for the inferno.

Reaching the park, I slid the car into the shade of a big cottonwood, set the handbrake, and attempted to calm my frazzled nerves by closing my eyes and taking a few deep breaths. After Joanne wrestled her enormous basket off the back seat, we headed to our spot on the wide arc of stony beach, away from the crowd clustered near the parking lot. Up against a rocky arm of the mountain that juts into the lake, we unfurled our blanket alongside a sun-bleached log.

Barefoot, I wobbled painfully across the rocky strand, arms jutting and body bending in all manner of contortions. At the lake edge, I waded in up to my waist—my body tensing in the frigid water—then lunged forward and swam out a few dozen strokes.

The haze was so thick that I could barely make out Harrison way off at the other side of the lake. I dog-paddled around, examined the drift of the smoke above the trees behind the beach. The wind was still in our favour, blowing from the south, away from the town and cove.

I caught sight of Joanne observing me, then quickly looking down to scribble something in her journal. Whenever she did this, I worried I was being analyzed. I kept checking too for signs that she had more than a friendly interest in me and was always relieved when I detected none. After that disastrous double date, she seemed to have gotten the memo. We just enjoyed spending time together whenever our schedules allowed.

Lessening any lingering relationship pressure that summer, she was regularly pulling double shifts at the resort while I was at Cultus Lake, bunked up with a crew four days a week building hiking trails. We planned to be together often in September, though. As soon as our summer jobs ended, we were bound for Vancouver. Her to school. Me, I wasn't yet sure. I had done poorly on my senior finals. Which meant university was, at least for the moment, out of the picture.

Wade was mostly out of the picture as well. The previous year, after he'd somehow managed to graduate high school, he hired on with a logging outfit up the lake at Silver River camp. He was a tree faller then, just as his father once was.

I did see Wade that May at Sandy Cove, one of the few beaches on the otherwise stony lakeside where you can lounge comfortably. The weather still too chilly for swimming, Joanne and I were picnicking there with some friends.

I broke with my usual caution to ogle him openly. I couldn't believe his transformation. From eight months on heavy inclines—lugging hefty industrial chainsaws and bucking downed trees—his body had bulked up and fairly burst his T-shirt, a more muscled version of the mature look he has now.

He was bragging to these rough-looking types—other loggers, probably—about how in the fall he'd be working some high-paid gig for his uncle in Montreal. According to Joanne, that wasn't what he had explained to Maureen. She believed his trip east was a peace offering from his mom to her estranged family—a one and done before he and Maureen got married.

As it turned out, not even Wade knew what course he was going to take. His swaggering around that day quite scared me, so I only nodded once but never asked about his plans. At our senior prom later that month, I finally mustered the nerve—which ended in harsh words and a scuffle. I hadn't seen him since.

At the park that August afternoon, Joanne was propped against the log, stretched out on our blanket, reading. She was always so interested in things, ready to research topics, jot thoughts down. That was why she'd received top marks in our graduating class. As for me, in senior year I just didn't see the point of school anymore. With what I really desired off the table, I lost interest in things. I found it difficult to get out of bed in the morning and lay there immobilized for hours, staring at the ceiling.

After swimming to shore, I hobbled past a teenage couple sprawled on a blanket, kissing. A shirtless man skipping rocks on the water. By then, I'd wearied of guiltily stealing glances at guys and was not quite so cowardly in my gawking. I noted how the curly hair on his bare chest faded into his tan. How it reappeared a shade darker just below his navel, only to be obscured under the beltline of the khakis that hung loosely off his hip bones.

Reaching our blanket, I retrieved the towel draped over the log and dried my shivering body. "Whoever says the water is warmer over here is nuts." My teeth chattered as I motioned with my chin to the lake, at bits of charred wood bobbing in the shallows. "If the wind whips around, the fire could head this way."

Joanne squinted up at me. "Maybe we should head back, then."

"Nah, we're okay for now."

I marvelled at all the books and magazines she had spread out on our blanket. I've always prided myself in being an avid reader, but my affinity for books back then was nothing compared to Joanne's, or my mother's. They read two or three tomes at the same time. I couldn't even guess how they kept the storylines from jumbling together.

Along with a copy of *Lolita* open on Joanne's lap, on the blanket beside her lay a thin paperback with the word HOWL in large black type on the cover. It partially obscured another, *Auntie Mame*. Within easy reach, a rock and pen restraining its pages from flipping in the breeze, her journal concealed yet another paperback. I slipped it out from under the notebook, skimmed through the pages. "What's this one?"

Bonjour Tristesse. Joanne pronounced the title with obvious relish. "It's about this teenager who lives with her father and a run of his mistresses on the French Riviera." With a finger, she nestled behind her ear a strand of blond hair that had disengaged from her ponytail. "Can you imagine that kind of thing happening around here?"

I pondered the question a moment and, as it had done years earlier—the day Wade and I met on the river—my new life in Vancouver called to me. The distant foghorns proclaiming what was to come: boyfriends, sex, something to do that I loved. Everything I now have, though blessedly not in the manner I then envisioned it.

"Well," I said, "I can imagine a lot happening. Only not here."

Her eyes widened mischievously. "Oh, Teddy. That's why I like you—you and your little baby face. When you're not being melancholy or morose, you have this sense there's something beyond." She indicated with a tilt of her head the lake and our little town across it obscured in smoke. "Anyway, I love the book, but it's depressing. The author was only eighteen when she wrote it."

"What's so depressing about that?"

"Look at what she'd already accomplished!" She flung her arms aside in mock exasperation. "And look at us. We're the same age. Have either of us got any novels—or anything, really—on the go?"

I laughed. "Stop torturing yourself. I'm sure there's enough material in that journal of yours for several books. And please don't call me baby face. You know how I hate that." I flicked her bare thigh with my towel.

"Ouch, Teddy. Don't be such a brat. I was only joking." She rummaged through the nearby pebbles and selected one to fling at me.

I dodged the missile, which clattered across the shingle at my back. "Besides, you've only just turned eighteen. You still have a whole year before you're over the hill."

Joanne stuck out her tongue, went back to reading *Lolita.*

I stretched out my long legs on the blanket, leaned against the log, and felt the sun warm my body. Retrieving my sunglasses, I surveyed the lake, then along the beach. A low stone wall separated it from the brief strip of mown grass that provided level ground for picnic tables and barbecue pits. Behind the lawn and adjacent parking lot, moss and fern ascended abruptly into the forested mountain.

In the shade under tall cedar, fir, and cottonwood, a smattering of people ate at wooden tables while others in folding chairs read or played cards. At the lake edge, kids in inner tubes splashed about in the water. Everyone was seeking relief from the unusually dry heat that all that month had engulfed the southern half of the province. Most were locals or from a few miles around, but some cars displayed licence plates of other provinces or the States.

My gaze ran back along the beach. The waves of heat radiating from the pebbles made it a dreamlike scene, everything appearing in slow motion. The young lovers gathered up their blanket and sauntered toward the parking lot. Sunglasses shading his eyes, the man who had been skipping rocks wandered into the water, his pant legs rolled up past his knees.

Lifting my arms, I crossed the index finger and thumb of both hands, forming a rough rectangle. Bringing it to my left eye while closing my right, I narrowed the frame to contain only Joanne's face, then broadened it to include her hand scrawling something in the journal and, finally, her entire slim figure.

Shifting my sights to the lake, I searched for the thin line of our resort town that defines the boundary between water and mountains. But I found that, as if in a dense fog, it had been erased.

I let my attention drift back to Joanne, then redirected it along the shore—halting abruptly at the bare-chested fellow. He turned and stood with his back to the lake, observing us, his broad-shouldered torso silhouetted against the plane of the water.

I was relishing my new-found brazenness when gawking at other men. Even so, I was startled at having been caught spying. I quickly lowered my hands and pivoted toward Joanne, who was again scribbling in her journal. "I think that guy is staring at us."

"What guy?"

"That guy over there."

"I don't think he's staring at *us*, Teddy." She lowered her pen, smiling in that way she has of holding her mouth so I'm sometimes not sure if she's kidding. "He's probably wondering what you're doing looking through your fingers. I sure would." She chuckled. "Oh, he's coming this way."

The man stopped a few paces off. Towering over us, he smiled broadly. Even taller than me and solidly built, he appeared to be in his early thirties. Light and shadow danced along his shoulders, biceps, spread over his chest.

Removing his sunglasses, he took me in. "Hi. I was wondering if you two live in the area?"

Joanne briefly scrutinized the man, then beamed back at him. She indicated Harrison, invisible through the haze. "Why, we live right over there."

"Are there any good places in town to eat? Other than the resort. Their prices are a little rich for me."

"Sure. There are a number of restaurants I'd recommend." She fetched her pen and notebook, jotted a few names, ripped out the page, and presented it to him.

He scanned the list, slipped it into his pants pocket. "Thanks, that'll be a great help." Then shifting his focus to me, he extended his hand. "I'm David, by the way."

Lusting after handsome men in secret was one thing; encountering them close range in the wild was more difficult. And though in Grade 10 we boys had been taught the art of the firm handshake, I couldn't muster the courage to respond to him. I gaped instead at the stones alongside my blanket.

Joanne scowled at me, then reached over and slid her hand into David's to accept his greeting. "I'm Joanne, and the daydreamer over there is Teddy."

I glanced up, managed to give him a nod, which he returned.

"Such a beautiful spot," he said. "Too bad there's so much smoke. Have you both lived here long?"

"My parents and I moved here a few years ago," Joanne said. She twiddled her fingers in my direction. "He's lived here since the Precambrian."

Just as I had earlier with Wade, I marvelled at the familiarity in which Joanne dealt with others. Her father was the manager of our town's tony resort, where my dad worked as a groundskeeper. In hotel management, relocating every few years is apparently the norm. This nomadic existence had caused her to feel like an outsider, she had once told me, but it had also given her a wider perspective.

"What about you?" Joanne said. "Where are you from?"

"Seattle."

"Oh," she said, a note of triumph in her voice. "We've been there *many* times. My mom and me, I mean. Not Teddy. He never goes anywhere." Once again, she dismissed me with a flip of her hand, then gave a short laugh. I lowered my eyes to my lap as the man examined me.

Joanne continued. "So, what brings you to our neck of the woods?"

David hesitated, then replied, "Summer holidays. Getting away from it all."

"How long are you here for?"

"I'm not sure. Maybe a few days. So peaceful. And pretty. Except for the smoke, of course. But there are fires everywhere this time of year, it seems." David eyed the books and magazines haloed around Joanne. "You two sure look like big readers."

With a sly grin, Joanne fished a book out of her basket and held it up. "Oh, yes, we both are, and this is what *he's* taking sooo long to read."

I attempted to grab for the book, but Joanne was too quick. Laughing, she pointed to its title, *Peyton Place*. "Look how he's dog-eared the pages at all the juicy parts. Don't you hate people who do that?"

David chuckled. "Actually, I finished it recently. I never knew small-town life could be so ... interesting." Again, he addressed the comment to me. Grinning, he sat beside me on the log. "So, what do you two do other than swim in that cold water and read?"

Joanne chucked the book back into her basket. "I'm working for the summer at the resort, but in the fall I'll be attending university in Vancouver."

Drawing up my legs, I hugged my knees to my chest. "Same here," I said, although, of course, it wasn't entirely true.

"What was that you were doing with your hands, Teddy?" David asked. "You were holding them up to your eyes."

"Oh, it's just something a teacher showed me—to help compose photos."

Clumsily mimicking my gesture, David circled the fingers of one hand, holding the tube they made to his right eye. Blue grey, like mine, I couldn't help noticing.

"This way?" he said.

"More like this." I peered up at him through the frame made by the thumb and index fingers of both hands.

Bending down, David did the same, and for a moment we gazed into one another's eyes.

"It ... it helps you focus ... eliminate details," I stammered, unsettled by being observed so intently. Strangely, it sparked an opening, allowing me the nerve to stare through my fingers at his nipple—a brown disc on a muscled plane. Immediately, my cheeks flushed, my eyes darted away. I broke the frame and resumed clutching my knees to my chest.

Joanne studied David, then returned her attention to me. She appeared about to speak but said nothing.

"Interesting." David's framed eye swept past me out to the water, then back again to my face. His hands dropped lazily across his chest, before hanging at his thighs. "Do you own a camera?"

I shook my head no.

With the back of his hand, David wiped beads of perspiration from his forehead. "Okay, I don't mean to be presumptuous, but it really is hot. Would you guys like a pop or a beer? I've got some in the trailer that should be chilled by now."

"I'd love a pop," said Joanne, already packing her books in her basket.

Hitched to a turquoise Pontiac sedan was one of those streamlined aluminum trailers that resembles a bullet or a bomb. It was parked under an ancient cedar, and I noted how a huge branch—another trunk, really—veered away from the main tree at a right angle before curving upward toward the sky.

Inside the trailer, it was cooler than I had expected. The result, I supposed, of being stationed all morning in the shade of the big tree. I was surprised too at how roomy the interior was. It sported a small kitchen, a table with benches on either side. To the right an unmade, elevated bed. At the back, beyond the kitchen, a heavyset man in a sweat-stained T-shirt and rumpled shorts sat up on the lower of two bunks. Hoisting his legs off the bed, he stood unsteadily and lurched toward us.

David introduced us to Jack. A man in his forties, bleary-eyed and smelling of cigarette smoke, with a beer belly and the breath to match. David suggested his friend go outside for some fresh air instead of being cooped up, drinking in the trailer all day.

Jack mumbled, "What fresh air?"

After rummaging in a small fridge, David presented some bottles, asked what we would like. Joanne selected a Coke and the rest of us beer. We arranged ourselves around the table—Joanne next to David, Jack sliding in beside me. He collapsed against my shoulder, his leg swung wide, squeezing into mine. To keep away from him and the stale smell of his body, I crowded against the wall, only for him to inch over and crush into me again.

When David caught sight of this, he scowled at his friend, rapped his fingertips on the tabletop. Jack shrank away from me at the prompt.

Joanne looked askance at this little scene, but quickly masked her discomfort with one of her gracious smiles. "What do you do for a living, David?"

"You're a teacher," I said.

He gaped at me in surprise. "Yeah, eighth grade. Is it that obvious?"

"The questions. Summer holidays. Just a hunch. What do you teach?"

"Math. Science."

I groaned, lengthening the sound for effect. "My worst subjects."

"I'm sure you have other talents," he said with a nervous laugh. "I hope you don't start looking at me as if I've come from outer space."

Jack snorted, abruptly rose to his feet, said he'd drink his beer outside. I was relieved when he was gone; he seemed both agitated and in a daze. I was thinking Jack was the one more likely from outer space when David said, "Don't mind him. He's harmless. It's just ... the heat is really getting to him."

David regarded Joanne sheepishly, then across the table his gaze lingered on me. A smile broke again across his face. "It's unusual to find young people taking so strongly to books. Are your parents readers?"

"Both our mothers are," said Joanne. "Mine has a huge collection. She travels to Toronto whenever she can and brings back all kinds of offbeat books. That's how I got *Howl* and *Lolita*."

I was about to remind Joanne that my mother had read *Lolita* a year ago and she checked it out from the public library, but I held back when I noticed David raising an eyebrow.

"Toronto," he said. "That's a long way."

"Well, usually she only goes to Vancouver or Seattle." She peered at David through batted lashes, her habit of attempting to endear herself to everyone she met. "Mom grew up in Toronto and misses it. All her friends are there."

From a pack on the table I jostled out a cigarette, and with the lighter next to it, David sparked a yellow flame. I exhaled a column of smoke, pushed the pack toward him, but he waved it away. "Those are Jack's."

"Actually, my mother's a frustrated artist," Joanne said. "She says she needs the culture of the big cities to inspire her—calls this place a 'waterlogged cultural desert.' Once she took me along to Toronto. We had such fun going to fancy restaurants, parties with people she knows, who are all painters and authors."

"And your dad? Does he go too?" David directed the question to Joanne while peeking over at me.

"No," she said. "All he does is work. For some reason he adores it here. They fight about it all the time."

Next, Joanne would be telling David about the prescription pills her mother took when she was restless and angry. About the others she employed for depression, for controlling her weight. I had heard all this before, and, because the beer had gone right to my bladder, I made my excuses, wedged myself into the trailer's cramped washroom, and pissed.

When I returned Joanne was jotting something in her journal while David schooled her about Toronto—its museums, theatres, and clubs.

"We've been there on several occasions recently," he said.

"You and Jack?" I said.

"No," he laughed. "Not Jack. Someone else."

I scowled. "So who's Jack?"

"Jack's just ... an old friend."

Joanne gawped at her watch, her lips pouted, her eyes suddenly wide. "Oh my gosh, I've forgotten all about the time. I have to be at work in half an hour." Extending her hand, she smiled at David. She said she hoped her stories about her mother weren't a bore.

"Not at all," he said, smiling broadly while slipping his fingers in hers in farewell. His eyes darted to mine, and, though he refrained from shaking my hand, he mentioned that if I was free later, I should come back for another beer.

My face flushed with a rush of excitement, but, ever the ingenue, I turned aside so as not to look at him and replied haltingly, "Maybe ... Dunno. Not sure Dad'll let me have the car."

As I drove back to town, I sensed Joanne scrutinizing me yet again. "You were awfully quiet back there," she said. "Quieter than you usually are. How come?"

"I don't know."

"Didn't you like him?"

"He was okay."

"Oh, I just want to shake you," she cried, making me grip the steering wheel and flinch. "I thought he was charming. God, how can you be so ... complacent all the time?"

"Detached."

"Fine, detached. Whatever you want to call it, the difference between you and me is that I want to *howl*." From the stack of paperbacks between us, she retrieved Ginsberg's book with the same word emblazoned on the cover and chucked it in my lap.

I laughed—my usual feint to deflect from my nervousness—a little too forcibly that time, the car veering briefly onto the shoulder of the twisty lakeside road. She could complain all she wanted, but being detached was second nature to me by then. I'd had to conceal my feelings for so long. Even from Joanne, at times. And Wade. Especially Wade.

"What?" she said. "Are you getting your shorts twisted because David might be *that way* and actually like you? If you truly are going with me to Vancouver, you're bound to meet all sorts. Better get used to it."

"Jesus, Joanne. What's the big deal. He's just some guy."

"I'm not talking about David. I'm talking about you. And do you even have a plan for the fall?"

"I'll get a job. Make up those exams. Something. I don't know."

"See, this is just what I'm talking about. You say you want to get out of this place, have a new kind of life, but instead you withdraw. Or smoulder." She regarded me, a worried expression on her face. "You do, you know, Teddy. And one day you're going to flare up and explode, like those fires up there." She motioned to the mountains behind her. "Or worse, you'll chicken out and be stuck here for the rest of your life."

I was as eager to leave for Vancouver as she was, and driving down that twisty blacktop, I pictured what might be in store—wandering alone along Kits Beach, say—far from that ideal experience I'd fantasized. Rather, alone and lonely, greedily eyeing the bodies of men lying beside their girlfriends, walking on eggshells, keeping up a pretense of having fun with my new friends. Dating girls, deceiving them.

And I understood that, while I had at last escaped the isolation of my stony tower, I was moving out into the world as if I were walking the plank. The width of that rough and weathered timber represented my experience, so arid and thin. On either side of this strip, the expanse from which I was excluded, inhabited by other young people having adventures with sex and relationships. At the end of the plank, those murky depths, the utter finality of all I'd ever been. No reference points, no signs or signposts to guide me. No book or magazine. No one else like me.

Back in town, Joanne told me to drop her at the hotel. She would shower and change in the staff quarters. I idled the car at the front gate, where the guard beamed at Joanne but glowered at me. He was suspicious ever since some of us village boys had been caught on the grounds, arranging the statues of Greek gods and goddesses in compromising positions.

It was one of the few times my easygoing father ever lost his temper with me. And though I was aware Mother thought the statues silly and pretentious, she gave me a stern warning about putting our family's livelihood in jeopardy.

"I'm sorry I was so hard on you back there," Joanne said at the staff entrance before stepping out of the car. "I don't think you will, but you should go back to the park later."

"I don't know."

"Go, Teddy. I can tell David's a gentleman. He won't pull anything weird, and he'll keep that creep Jack in check. You need to have some fun. You've been moping around ever since Wade took off to the camp."

When I arrived at our family's little house near the lakeside, my mother was just coming in from weeding the back garden. She unlaced her sun hat and tossed it on the kitchen table, blew aside the strand of grey that had fallen into her face. There was an oddball quality to that face. About the eyes, principally, that seemed to look so directly at the world they gave the impression of being at the point of crossing—which they thankfully never did.

"Damned buttercups, they get into everything. Worse than dandelions." She frowned at me, furrowing her brows. "And the grass, Mister, sure could use a good cutting." Then her face broke into a smile. "How was the water?"

"Cold as ever," I said. "Joanne doesn't bother going in anymore."

"And how is the dear?"

"Oh, you know ..."

My mother was careful not to appear too inquisitive about my friendship with Joanne. She assumed we were going together, and I offered nothing that might dissuade her. I wanted to give her that. Having failed my senior finals, Mother fretted that I would abandon my plans of furthering myself—just as she had when she married my father. It comforted her to think the resort manager's studious daughter was dating the underachieving son of its groundskeeper, correcting his sloppy grammar and improving his vocabulary.

I was surprised by how quickly the two of them had become friends. Mother kept people at arm's length, feigning interest and so never having much success winning them over. She left that sort of thing to my father.

What allowed her to break this cycle with Joanne was the fact they were both such voracious readers. The birds of a feather constantly exchanged books and got into long-winded discussions. I often had to haul Joanne away from Mother just to make it on time to wherever we were going.

Once Joanne asked me—only half kidding, I suspected—if I would like to trade moms.

Mother gestured to the envelope lying next to her sun hat on the kitchen table. "This came for you today."

"What is it?" I said, turning the package over in my hand and examining the Vancouver return address.

She tilted her head to one side and shot me a playful grin.

I tore open the manila envelope and pulled out a slim book with the title *The Spice-Box of Earth* printed on the cover above a grainy photo of the author. "Who's Leonard Cohen?"

Mother cocked one eyebrow.

Though I would come to pride myself on being a Canadian artist—a keen supporter of our cinema and theatre—at that time Mother was always taking me to task for knowing all about American singers and movie stars but nothing about our own artists.

"A Montreal poet," she answered. She slipped the book from my hands and traced her fingers over the cover photo of the clean-shaven young man. "He reminds me of you."

"Oh? How's that?"

"He's an old soul."

"I never know what that means."

"Not sure I do either, but seems about right." She passed me back the book. "It's your birthday present. Eighteen. Just imagine. You're a man now."

"My birthday isn't until next month."

"Your pre-birthday, then," she said. "The real present's coming later. I just thought you'd find this interesting."

"Mom, you shouldn't be spending our hard-earned money." I pecked her on the forehead and asked what she was making us for supper.

She wrinkled her nose. "It's too hot to cook, Teddy. When Dad gets home, why don't we pick up burgers and drive to the lake to watch the fires?"

So, that was what we did. Sitting in the back of our Studebaker, it was as if I were at a drive-in watching a double bill, only the two movies all at once. One, the flames and towers of smoke across the water. The other, my parents eating their burgers and chips.

From what I pieced together, their early love affair had been intensely romantic. Perhaps because they were far into middle age when they met—one sunset at Vancouver's Locarno Beach, where my father was a lifeguard and my mother swam after work nearly every summer evening. The handsome Irishman certainly swept away my mother, for after only a few weeks of his blarney, she abandoned her career as a private secretary and married him. So, that evening, I imagined the two of them going into a clinch—the music swelling, the camera tracking in on their faces silhouetted against the leaping flames.

But of course their talk wasn't about *moon and June*, but a back-and-forth about how much larger the fire appeared and what we ought to do if it jumped to our side of the lake and got close to the house.

After some moments of this, Dad twisted around in his seat, his eyes fixed sternly upon mine. "Son, they could soon be calling up all the able-bodied men to fight the fire."

He barely registered, though. The half-eaten hamburger cold in my hands, my mind drifted off. A shadow skimming the water's surface. To the park, the parking lot beyond the stony beach. To the silver trailer in the shelter of the ancient cedar.

My father allowed me to keep the car that evening. So, by seven—with Mother's reminder that I had to wake up early the next morning for work—I was heading back to the park. To calm my nerves over what I was getting myself into, I fiddled with the radio. Only waves of static from a Vancouver station, intermingled with a few bars of a Johnny Mathis song.

The wind had changed direction, blowing toward the park. I stepped out of the car to find that most of the swimmers and picnickers had already fled to the safety of the town. Only a spatter of vehicles and trailers remained in the smoke-filled lot, David's among them.

I shuffled down to the beach, where, because of my nervousness, two clumsy attempts were required to light a cigarette. Flicking away the match, it spat as it struck the surface of the lake. Though the sun had yet to dip behind the western mountains, the light through the haze was already failing.

As was my resolve. My body recognized what it wanted, but my mind, as always, threw up obstacles. Perhaps I'd misread David's glances and suggestive remarks. Perhaps his friendliness was only the habit of a popular middle-school teacher. I reached into my pocket for my keys and turned to go.

"Hello again. I thought it might be you," David said, striding from the parking lot across the water's stony margin. "I'm glad you could come back."

Again, he offered his hand. I overcame my reluctance and shook it. David's grip was strong and surprisingly warm. I pulled away before he loosened his grasp. Jostling a cigarette from my pack, I presented it to him, then recalled from the afternoon that he didn't smoke.

He grinned. "There's enough smoke getting in my eyes already."

"Where's Jack?"

"In the trailer, passed out. Snoring. He had a few too many again."

We were quiet for a moment, listening to the water lapping the rocky shore.

I expelled smoke out the side of my mouth, away from him. "He was awfully friendly this afternoon."

Discomfort flickering across his face, David shook his head. "I'm sorry. He shouldn't have bothered you. I had no idea he was so far gone. Not to excuse him, but he's had a rough few months." He paused, as if wondering whether to reveal more. "His wife's divorcing him. She's even gone to court to keep him from his children."

Such custody battles were all too common for us at the time. But then, it puzzled me how Jack's behaviour—his boorishness, his sloppy appearance—could result in a punishment so severe. In my teenage self-absorption, I had no interest in inquiring further about David's friend. Still, as we navigated the rocky shore, I sensed the pressure building from the many other things I wanted to ask.

On the strip of grass bordering the parking lot, we sat side by side on a picnic table's bench. Threading another cigarette from my pack, I lit it with the one I was about to extinguish, then gazed at the shoreline. In the blankness beyond, in my mind's eye, across the lake I saw the Harrison River begin its journey to the Fraser.

The image triggered, as it so often did, that moment three years before. Of being caught in the current while swimming off the log boom. And seated with that by all appearances kind and thoughtful man, I felt again I was in danger. Not only from where our meeting might lead, but from the sudden necessity I felt to confess to him.

In fits and starts, I recounted how I was sucked under the frigid river that day. How something sinister had seemed to lurk in its depths. That, panicked, overcome by the current, it took all my strength to keep from being swept away. That, for a while, I feared I might drown.

As I stared at the smoky haze, David hoisted one leg and straddled the bench. I was aware of him studying me, as if trying to read what underlay my story. "The best thing is to let yourself go with the current, Teddy," he finally said, "and to work your way gradually into shore."

I failed to comprehend the full weight of our clumsy, coded language, but sensed something essential was being conveyed—and a correspondence, too, deeper than I'd ever felt with Wade. David and me, outliers on a lakeside bench, fumbling toward each other.

I pivoted sideways and found him staring at the grass at his feet, head slightly cocked. Suspecting again that he was weighing whether or not to say more, I turned back to the grey expanse and waited.

"You can end up far from where you started," he said at last, his voice straining to deliver the deeper meaning, "but it can save your life."

My hand trembled. I hurled the cigarette onto the rocky shore. Where it landed, a plume of smoke erupted. "My life ... I have some things I need to figure out about my fucking life."

"What things?" he said, almost in a whisper.

Tears welled up, as they did so readily. I desperately needed to speak honestly, and yet, never having done so, I was only able to shield my eyes with my hand as if to discern something cloaked in the smoke over the lake. "I need to figure out ..." I abandoned the ruse and lurched to my feet. "I just need to get away from here. Experience new things."

David stood, rested his hand on my shoulder. "Are you okay?"

"Yeah, yeah," I said. Throat constricted, my voice shook. "It's just ... this fucking smoke."

I struggled free of the bench and bolted to the low stone wall that marked the transition from the park to the rocky strand. He slipped in behind me. So close, through my thin shirt I sensed heat radiating off his body.

"Are you still upset about Jack? Is that it?"

I shook my head. I fumbled in my pocket for another cigarette. Reaching his arms around to encircle me, he cradled my hand in his. "You don't need another one of those."

I gaped down at our fingers touching, felt myself stiffen below.

Headlights flashed through the trees. I broke from David's embrace, and when I composed myself enough to look, I found an RCMP patrol car pulling into the lot. We hurried over, and the officer informed us that flares had been spotted nearby. They were evacuating the area, he said, eyeing the Airstream beside us. We would have to find somewhere else to stay for the night.

I told David I would lead him to a trailer campsite in town. It was owned by Maureen Taylor's parents, who lived with her in a small house on the property. As I drove along the twisting road, the familiarity of the terrain comforted me—the overarching branches, the glimpses of the glassy lake. But I was gut punched each time I caught sight of David behind me in his Pontiac, his eyes in the rear-view mirror fixed on mine.

By the time we pulled into the campsite, registered, and hooked up, it was almost dark. David and I hesitated just outside the trailer door, and although we stood close, the gap between us seemed immense. I told him I should be on my way and spun around as if to leave.

"Wait. Don't go."

Again, I sensed a tentativeness in David, but just then I wasn't on edge. Something had shifted, and I felt tenderness for him as I witnessed him fumbling for words.

"You know ... you know what you told me about wanting to have new experiences?"

A smile pulled at my lips at the clumsiness of his proposition. I understood what he was asking, what he was offering. I was elated the moment had finally arrived—over where it would lead, if I only allowed it.

I confronted the trailer door. "What about Jack?"

David nudged it open. "Jack's been crashed out for hours in his bunk. He's out cold for the night."

After hesitating a moment, I took the trailer's steps in a single stride.

At the open windows, the curtains emitted a soft light. Through the plaid cloth, the smell of grilling hamburgers, the laughter of families at nearby campsites.

I took a seat on the edge of his bed, my hands frozen in my lap, my breathing constrained. David eased himself onto the mattress beside me, slowly unbuttoned my shirt, and peeled it off my shoulders. He paused, a look of admiration and urgency playing across his face. He pressed his hand into my chest, closed his eyes, and took a deep breath. Gently, he prompted me to lie back on the rumpled sheets.

An unexpected feeling coursed through my body. Sexual, yes, but I experienced another kind of yearning as well. Not for that man, exactly, or other men, even Wade. But it was as if I were being carried downriver again by that powerful current, only I was surrendering. The water buoying me, I was drawn toward another shore, as yet far off. The tension from having to suppress my feelings these past years drifting away.

David asked if I was all right. I nodded yes.

"Your body's so taut," he said. "Almost like stone."

Our lips touched, but I barely returned his kiss. All my awareness lay in my cock. My eyes closed. His tongue lapped a trail of moisture down my chest. Lips stuttered across my stomach. Fingers unbuckled my belt. I came right away when he touched me.

As I stared at the ceiling, he pressed his length against me, his hand resting lightly on my chest. I sensed myself drifting toward my destination, and my speech, though seeming to come from that still distant place, was clear, its meaning no longer expressed in ciphers. "Your life ... what is your life like?"

"It's okay now. More than okay. I have someone. And I get to meet people I would otherwise likely never know. Some wonderful, some not." Propping himself on one elbow to better view me, he traced circles with his fingertips on my stomach. "I realize now things aren't always what they seem."

I twisted onto my side to face him, looking him in the eyes. "When did you start ...?"

"Your age, but it was always there. I won't lie. It was confusing, at first. But you figure it out as you go along. Then there's chance. Luck."

"Like this afternoon."

"Yes." A smile broke across his face, warmly colouring his voice. "Like this afternoon."

Sitting up, he quickly shucked off his pants and shorts to straddle my hips. Shaping a frame with the fingers of both hands, he gazed through it along the length of my body, lingering finally on my face. Not until I grinned did he smile again in return.

When he raised himself onto his knees, I manoeuvred my hand between his legs and began to stroke myself. He pulled my greedy arm away, spit in his fingers, reached behind him and took over. An almost unbearable pleasure pulsed through me. Slowly he guided me into him. I arched my hips. He bent forward. Pressing one hand into the mattress at my shoulder for support, he attended to himself with the other.

"That's it, that's it." He breathed in short gasps, his mouth half open, eyes half closed. When he came, he laughed, then lifted off me and, kneeling still, buried his face in my chest.

We rested a few minutes, motionless. I told myself this was the moment my life truly began. Then thoughts intruded. The four sweaty days of trailwork ahead. Mother at the kitchen table leafing through the poetry book. Dad seated nearby, casting worried glances at his watch.

I let David know I had to get home.

We were scrambling back into our clothes when I realized Jack wasn't snoring anymore. I turned to see him watching us from his bunk. He smirked and waved as David ushered me to the door.

Outside, a lamppost cast a semicircle of light onto the gravel pad beside the trailer. Nestled among the big firs, families gathered around picnic tables were chatting idly, their bright faces lit by the wicks of Coleman lanterns.

The embarrassment I felt at having been spied on by Jack gave way to awkwardness. Not knowing how to say goodbye. Shaking hands didn't seem enough. But to embrace? Right there in the campsite in front of everyone? David leaned toward me so that, for a moment, I thought he might.

Instead, he took my hand and, from behind his back, placed something in it. I peered down, startled to find a small camera. As I began to protest, David hushed me. "This is just an old one I keep around for backup. Use it, Teddy. Focus. Continue composing."

Inching closer, slipping his fingers into the opening of my pants pocket, he whispered in my ear, "Please, take some pictures."

I ambled along the gravel road that wound through the campsites, my body still thrumming from the sex, but also from finally putting down a marker on a new life. It was dark except for the faint light filtering through the trees from the few lampposts positioned around the site. The wind had increased, and the smoky air seemed less oppressive.

I was approaching Dad's car, when behind me I heard footsteps scuffling through the gravel. I twisted around to see a figure emerge from the darkness into a pool of lamplight.

Wade.

Lit as he was from above, hard shadows drawn under each brow obscured the expression in his eyes. I was immediately on guard. He had roughed me up at our senior prom in May, and from his broad stance and hunched shoulders, he appeared similarly aggressive then. In my nervousness, I found it difficult to come up with anything to say, blurting out finally, "What're you doing here?"

He glowered at me. "I have a girlfriend who lives here. Maureen. Remember?"

That didn't wash with what Joanne had been told two weeks before. Maureen used quite a few choice words to describe how—after Wade delivered the news he planned to remain in Montreal—she drove to his family's farm, poured lighter fuel on his precious letter jacket, and set it aflame in the front yard.

Wade strode toward me, and I cowered back a couple of paces. "Thought you were up the lake," I said.

"Evacuated." He cleared his throat and spat into the nearby cedars. "Better question is: What are *you* doing here?"

"I ... met some guys at that new park who needed a campsite for the night. They couldn't stay there because of the fire."

"Guys," he repeated.

"Yeah, two. Met them this afternoon when Joanne and I were over there swimming."

When he took another step toward me, I managed to hold my ground.

"Seems pretty quick for him to be giving you something expensive like that," he said.

I peered down at David's gift cradled in my hand.

"Sure a long time in there with the lights off too," he said.

"You spying on me?"

Grown accustomed to the dark, I read his unblinking stare, his handsome face marred by that habitual grimace.

He whipped around, stormed off, the rocks crunching under his boots puncturing the silence.

I gaped after him—the cold swagger exciting me even then, the tight jeans, the T-shirt moulded by his muscled torso. I was still pissed at him for how he had treated me at the prom, and that anger rushed to the surface. My jaw clenched. "Wade!" I called out, just loud enough for him to hear.

He halted. Turned.

"You asshole," I said, my voice catching. "You fucking asshole."

Then I aimed my new camera straight at his head.

Part 2

I have seen the holy places though I never knew it.
I have travelled on, not knowing all my life that the
mecca of my pilgrimage has been reached so young,
and that all after was the homeward journey.
—JOHN METCALF, "The Years in Exile"

sea change

LET ME FAST-FORWARD nine months. May 1960. Some Sunday evening: I don't recall which. I do remember, for an inexplicable reason, the sound my red Keds made as I chased after the No. 9 bus. On the blacktop, a percussive thwack, a rat-a-tat-tat semblance of the intensity of life that I sorely lacked.

Chest heaving, hands cupped at my waist, I jerked to a halt and pouted after the sputtering yellow box disappearing around the bend. Way out there at Point Grey on a weekend schedule, there wouldn't be another bus for more than an hour. *Fuck it*, I told myself. I would hitch back downtown—though I wasn't really in a hurry. Nothing called to me there.

Grumbling at myself for not dressing for the city's habitual chill, I buttoned my shirt at the collar and hugged my chest. Below the fringe of threads dangling from my cut-off jeans, goosebumps pimpled my thighs.

Up ahead, a deserted stretch of Marine Drive skirted Burrard Inlet. Across the water, glimpses of North Van through a thick grove of trees. Slatted above the road, the sky was a curdled grey—a blanket of darkening clouds, threatening rain.

The afternoon, though, had begun sunny and warm.

I had taken the sparsely occupied noontime bus out to the university to visit Joanne. Since the previous September, we had both been living in Vancouver. She had almost completed her first year of a bachelor's program in English lit while I wasted away as an orderly in the bowels of Vancouver General, working the night shift on the TB unit. On free weekdays, I struggled through evening classes to make up high school subjects I had failed so disastrously.

That afternoon at the university was what passed for blessed relief from that plodding day-to-day. On the grassy strip of the East Mall, I tossed around a Frisbee with Joanne and her college pals. Their boisterous talk echoed off the nearby modernist buildings whose spare glass facades seemed to exclude the likes of poor me.

At the far west end of the mall, we hit the student union, a squat, Bauhaus-looking stucco concoction. Inside—its white walls and institutional furniture as sterile as the hospital where I was ungainfully employed—we drank our root beer and chatted amid the din of the other students.

Her friends were like a sampler box of pop culture. One was a handsome, goateed man in a black sportcoat, dress shirt, and skinny tie—a holdout from the Daddy-o generation. Another, a longhair in tie-dyed painter's pants, his kurta shirt speckled with tiny round mirrors puckered inside stitched hems. The cherry on top was the plaid-skirted, bobby socks girl, her V-neck sweater splayed open at a bright-red tie.

The two men in our group jockeyed for my attention, peppering me with questions, laughing at my feeble comic attempts.

The girl sighed loudly in counterpoint to each sweep of her hand, paging through a book she held upright to show off. Something unknown to me called *The Price of Salt*. She re-engaged when the subject around our little table turned, as it always did, to literature—this time written by authors I hadn't yet heard of. Baldwin, Capote, Vidal, and, the girl chirped in, Highsmith.

As differently as Joanne's friends were dressed, they all seemed to have the same opinions about these authors. Their outsider status, the students agreed, allowed them an enhanced perspective with which to comment on the American experience. In turn, this gave certain elements of their fiction a literary charge, a seriousness for readers who might otherwise have found them scandalous.

This oblique academic talk is so obvious to me now, but then it might as well have been ancient Greek. A little buzz, I remember thinking, would have improved my comprehension, a mickey of rum smuggled in to spike our chilled mugs.

As always, Joanne scrutinized me during the conversation, on that occasion gauging my response to what was, I later learned, a litany of queer authors. Surely she had suspicions about me, though they had never been voiced and I hadn't the nerve yet to confirm them.

Under a greying, dimpled sky, I said my goodbyes outside the union to the assorted hipsters, giving them a quick wave as a gambit to avoid shaking their hands. The good-looking beatnik eyed me earnestly, which was unsettling but faintly thrilling.

As I moved toward Joanne to chastely peck her on the cheek, she linked her arm in mine and steered me down the wide sidewalk in the direction of the inlet. "Why don't we talk a bit?"

I tensed instantly, my shoulders stiffening and levering upward. Her clipped, matter-of-fact delivery signalled another dressing-down or pep talk. It is still difficult to tell the one from the other.

"Okay, lay it on me," I said.

"Oh, stop acting like I'm your mother."

"My mother is way nicer."

"Your mother is a doll, but she won't tell it like it is. Only your best friend can do that, Teddy."

"Ted," I reminded her yet again. After relocating to the city, I had, once and for all, discarded the childishly sounding "Teddy" that dogged me into adulthood.

"Oh, yeah. Sorry. After all this time, it's hard to remember. Like I was saying, as your best friend ..."

"Come on, Joanne. I hardly see you these days."

"Which is sort of my point, buddy. You should be at the university too, where we can hang out all the time. Look, you're already a big hit. My friends obviously adore you."

"I don't know why. I barely said a word back there."

"You didn't need to. Not with that cute little baby face."

"Stop infantilizing me."

"Such a big word! You sound like a college man already. How about instead I use 'devilishly handsome'?"

"Besides," I said, "all of you are so busy with your seminars. Symposiums. Even if I was out here, I doubt you could find the time. I mean, what's an old friend compared to the semiotics of Foucault or whatever you're into now."

I attempted to wriggle out of her embrace, but she tugged me closer. "I promised myself, this time I wouldn't take the bait."

"What's so different today?"

"I'm worried about you, knucklehead."

"Look, Joanne. I'm busting my butt to get out here."

"I know you are. It's not that, really. You just ... I don't know, Ted. You seem so sad lately."

"I thought it was *detached*."

"Sorry, kiddo. Now it looks more like depressed." She leaned her head toward mine for a moment, then said, "How's your social life?"

When I moved to the city, I imagined having adventures meeting men—as I'd done with David at the beach. But working graveyard at the hospital, on top of my evening classes, sleeping till three most afternoons at my shabby boarding house—all I came across was the stream of tight-lipped backpackers and students there, short-timers impatient to clear out.

Except for occasional visits with Joanne and her nerdy bunch, my only other human contact was my strict landlady—sour tempered except when she was angling for a rent cheque—and the unhappy nurse who bossed around us orderlies without bothering to look up from her paperwork.

Joanne tugged me closer as we passed in silence under the tall gangling cedars, the end of the road approaching, the red octagonal sign there emblazoned with the white STOP. But how could I stop, veer from the only way I had ever known?

Even if I had found the courage to shift in a new direction, where would I have gone? As I later learned, there were ample bars and secret places for men like me, but with a life as constrained as mine, I wasn't aware of them. So I plodded the familiar alone until the cloud that followed me became as dark and clotted as those overhead that day.

Joanne halted at the sign where the road teed into Marine Drive and released me. After a kiss on my forehead, she stepped back. "Stop being so boo-hoo, kiddo. Do something, Teddy. I mean, Ted. Whoever you are."

I strode down Marine Drive, the maples and poplars thick and unruly on the inlet side. Marking the opposite border and mounting the university's low stone walls were cedar hedges, neatly trimmed, laced with the lighter-coloured leaves of grape and blackberry vines.

It began to mist. I shivered. Hurrying along the roadside, I cast backward glances, hoping to spot an oncoming car. And looking backward I thought of hitching with Wade.

From time to time, Wade's mom came across my mother at the Harrison Post Office where she was employed and had, despite her shyness, become the town crier. Before I could embargo any Wade news, Mother passed on how he was working in Montreal and living with his mom's family, how proud his mom was of his greatly improved French.

The clouds had blackened, and suddenly they let loose a torrent of rain. By the time I reached Spanish Banks, my clothes were soaked through, water sloshing inside my Keds at every footstep.

A Buick Riviera whizzed by, spitting a rooster tail of water behind it. I stuck out my thumb, but it passed me. A few minutes later, it overtook me again from the opposite direction. Inside the fogged-up windows was a shadowy figure.

I came upon the car parked in a small lot bordered on the inlet side by a thick stand of cedar. As I approached, the passenger window glided down to reveal a short bespectacled fellow—middle-aged, possibly older—leaning over the seat to speak through the open frame.

"You look wet," the man said.

I was about to make some snide comment about his stating the obvious when I noted the trembling in his voice as he spoke again. "I was driving home from work," he said, looking down but shooting me repeated glances over his wire-rimmed glasses. "And I saw you."

Punctuating the silence that followed, the sound of the surf lumbering onto the nearby shore, the click of the latch as he opened the passenger door a crack. "Would you like ... to get out of the rain?"

I hugged myself tighter and shivered more intensely. Listening to the rhythmic thumping of the wipers, I watched them swipe clean the view of the car's interior, only to relinquish it moments later to the pebbled streaks of rain.

"Sure, but just to get out of this mess." After lowering myself onto the seat next to him and closing the door behind me, I said, "This isn't what you think."

"Oh? What do I think, I wonder."

I shifted uncomfortably in my seat at this odd remark and fingered the door handle, ready to jump ship any moment. "I just need to get out of the rain, man."

My companion flicked a switch, and warm air spread up my bare legs. I shook my head *yes* when he opened a pack of Player's, tugged a cigarette partway out. I noticed the silver wedding band glinting in the light of the flame. *Another closet case*, I thought. *Just like me.*

The man tossed the pack onto the centre console without taking a cigarette for himself. I inhaled deeply, doubled over suddenly, coughing up a cloud of smoke. I shivered again, beginning to feel quite ill. Afraid of being rousted back out onto the street, I tried to stifle another round of hacking but failed, covering my mouth poorly with my hand and sputtering on the dash.

"It appears you're coming down with something." The man's voice was tinged not with annoyance as I had expected but with concern. "We better get you home and into some dry clothes."

I rolled down the window and tossed the unspent cigarette, smelling the rising tide, the kelp mouldering on beachsides. Through the tunnel of trees, tankers hunkered in the inlet—their rust-red bulks and their multicoloured cargo containers contrasting with the dark-green mass of the coastal mountains on the opposite side.

"Where do you live?" he said, backing his car onto the road.

"Fairview, but you can drop me anyplace downtown." I would catch a bus from there.

"I don't mind driving you home. It's more or less on my way."

The road took a sharp right at Locarno Beach, the place where my parents had met. I wondered what they would think of me now, getting picked up by some older man. I shuddered again as much from apprehension as from the cold.

Except for the one experience with David, nothing in my young life had prepared me for that moment. "Chance," David had said. "Luck." That unattractive, flabby, middle-aged man was my luck that day, I guessed. I expected him to make a move—a hand on my knee, a squeeze of my biceps—but none came. I couldn't tell if I was relieved or disappointed.

Across the road behind him, lights from the commercial buildings in Kitsilano squiggled in the increasing rain.

"I'm Randall, by the way."

"Ted," I said.

"Are you a student?"

I shook my head. "No. Not at the university, anyway."

He cast a quick look in my direction. I was painfully aware of my rumpled, yellowed shirt, my frayed cut-offs, so in contrast to his snappy clothes. A stylish black leather jacket and broad-striped grey pants. A green silk shirt, the space at its open collar encroached by silver chest hair.

"Lots of scholarship students out at UBC," he said. "I'm a professor. If you were wondering. Business Administration and Finance."

What a drag, I remember thinking then. Another wannabe hipster in arty-farty clothes but digging what he taught, a total square. My interest in him deflated a notch.

The restaurants and dry cleaners along the commercial strip gave way to low-slung apartment buildings, the sidewalks at their fronts edged with tall trees. The rain began to relent, the windshield wipers' thumping growing less insistent. In the silence at each interval, my stomach could be heard growling. Waking just before noon that day, I'd dashed out of the boarding house without eating, missing as I often did both breakfast and lunch.

"You're hungry," Randall said, his double-entry world view appearing—when it came to the basics—to sharpen his powers of perception. He announced that he would drive us to the Aristocratic, an all-night diner at the corner of Broadway and Granville.

Under its humming fluorescent lights, he appeared even shorter than I had taken him to be in the car—though in the booth opposite me he sat very erect in the way short people often do. One of his eyes drooped slightly as if that side of his body were falling asleep. His chubby face was almost comically plain, and curiously unlined for his age, which, despite his youthful manner and dress, I judged to be mid-sixties. With his wire rims and classy clothes, he resembled not so much a number cruncher but a writer or critic.

While I wolfed down a double cheeseburger, my thoughts turned back to Joanne, her friends at the student union, and the conversation earlier I'd found so impenetrable and coded. Dredging a fry through a puddle of ketchup, I said, "Have you heard of a writer named James Baldwin?"

A ridiculous question when viewed from my current vantage point, but as an isolated eighteen-year-old, my reading choices had been filtered through the prism of my mother's literary interests, who, Nabokov aside, suffered under the moral squeamishness of her day.

Randall smiled over his coffee cup. "Certainly. Why do you ask?"

"My girlfriend was talking about him earlier."

"Girlfriend?" Randall raised one eyebrow.

"She's an English major," I said, ignoring his inference. I hesitated to be more specific with this stranger, but with his ruddy face so earnest, his body so old and frail, in my state of ignorance it seemed foolish to distrust him. "She and her friends were talking about him earlier. And someone called Capote. And Vidal, I think it was."

This caused Randall to raise both eyebrows. "Authors of a certain type."

"Type?"

"Yes. Terribly au courant."

I sopped the last fry with ketchup, pushed the plate away. Balked at sorting through the layered implications to frame a more honest and personal question, one that honoured the terrible new field of play opening around me.

"You're a reader then, I take it," he said.

"Not so much anymore. With my night work and classes, I'm usually too bushed for anything else. Besides, I'm really more interested in art."

"Ah, you must be a painter. All the young men I meet seem to think themselves Picassos. Or are you, perhaps, a sculptor?"

"I can't afford anything like that. Just pencil sketches, though I've started working in watercolours."

"Your favourite artists?"

"I don't know, really. Pollock, maybe? Motherwell?"

"Oh, yes. Also my spouse's favourites."

I again noted the silver band glinting on his ring finger.

Outside the plate glass, the nightscape was streaked with light—refracted through the window of a laundromat opposite us, reflected off puddles in the street rippled by the gentle rain. And though he'd lent me his jacket, the chill pierced my clammy shirt.

"I've got an idea," Randall said, interrupting the silence by rapping his cup on the Formica tabletop. "Like I say, my place is more or less on the way. I own a very small Motherwell.

My partner insisted I buy it ages ago, before the artist became, well ... Motherwell. We could drop by and take a look."

My mouth crumpled into a frown. "You want to show me your etchings?"

He chuckled, a friendly mischievousness flashing in his eyes. "Only if you want."

What I wanted was as blurred as the buildings across the way. What I wanted wasn't an arty, old business prof. Yet there he was, filling that vacuum I called a life. His seeming kindness, his earnestness, his obvious need so like mine.

At Randall's twenty-third-floor West End apartment—the baggy sweatsuit he lent me drooping off my thin frame—my stomach did a flip as I spied through the big window the tiny people below strolling down the sidewalk, the toy cars zipping along the busy street. I'd never been up so high—except once on the observation deck of the Marine Building when my folks took me to Vancouver to see *The Red Shoes*.

What really impressed me wasn't that or the expansive view of English Bay and the North Shore lights blinking on but the long wall hung floor-to-ceiling with paintings.

Positioned next to what seemed to be a Blue Period Picasso—a listlessly staring woman hugging herself at the waist—was that small Motherwell. Its black squares contrasted with those in red and yellow on a flesh-coloured field. Neighbouring it was an early Pollock, his drip paintings prefigured in the jumble of abstract shapes.

My mouth agape, astonishment broke across my face. After recovering, I said, "They must have cost a fortune."

"Not so much as you'd think. We were very young when we bought these, or at least my partner was. Your age, I'd wager. And I haven't always been a lowly university professor."

Scattered among the canvases by the famous painters were others clearly inspired by the works, all signed by an artist I didn't recognize. R. Takahashi.

Randall stepped to a set of shelves that dominated the adjacent wall, tugged out a large art book. "Here, this might give you inspiration for your watercolours." He set in my hands a volume on Winslow Homer. "You can borrow it, if you want. As long as you like."

I took a seat on the sofa opposite the wall of paintings. The book fell open on a blue field interrupted by rough swaths of colour suggesting a long brown boat and two white sails under a bank of twisty tan clouds. "You can always come back later for more," he said.

My own cloud wrapped itself around me again, the sadness over feeling as if I didn't belong. I placed the book on the coffee table in front of me. Fearing I might burst into tears, I pushed it away, then took in his droopy eye. "Why are you being so nice?"

He shrugged, the corners of his mouth turned down. "Drink? You must drink, right? Seems half the kids your age attend my classes hungover."

He headed to a small cart by the doorway to the kitchen: bottles on its top shelf, tumblers below. He began to pour the liquor, then stopped. "How old are you, by the way?"

"I'll be nineteen in September."

"Most kids tell me they're twenty-one."

"Do I look twenty-one?"

"Maybe we better not, then. It might be unseemly."

"It's a little late to worry about that."

He chuckled and continued pouring the brown liquid into glasses. "Well, just the one, then." He seated himself next to me on the couch and placed my scotch and the bottle on the coffee table. "Because this is not what you think," he said with a wink.

I picked up the tumbler, swirled the contents, and gaped through it at this oddball shadowed in the peaty liquid.

"Not entirely, anyway," he said.

I felt myself tense. A rising hope, mingled with dread. "How do you mean?"

"Well, I confess when I first passed you, I did a double take and had to drive by again."

"Oh?"

"You have very beautiful legs, my friend."

I pulled away slightly and took a heavy nip from my drink.

"But when I saw you in the parking lot looking like a drowned cat—water running off your nose, your lashes—I felt something else."

"And what was that?"

"I don't know. Kinship, maybe. Empathy."

I was astonished at this remark. Worried again that I might cry, I downed the remaining contents of my glass, shoved the tumbler toward the bottle. I needed a boost to keep from drowning in the twisty implications.

"I don't think that's a good idea," Randall said. "It's 80 proof, you know."

I shrugged off the warning, poured myself another drink. By the third sip, my suspicion of his gentle questioning, his speaking to me as if we were already friends, dropped away. I opened up to him about my life. After an hour, I couldn't believe how much I'd confessed to him. About growing up in the Fraser Valley, working nights at the TB unit for nearly a year. About attending evening classes and living in the depressing boarding house. And confessing to him I hadn't a clue what I should do with my miserable life.

What made it so easy to reveal myself to him was that he seemed to know so much yet refrained from spoon-feeding me adult advice. He simply appeared interested in my life, prodding my revelations forward with more questions—his voice low, almost a whisper, soothing me. At last, my head drifting forward and my eyes starting to close, I watched him take the empty tumbler from my hand.

I woke to the sound of typing coming through an open door. It was followed by panic, my mind casting about for clues as to where I was. Slowly, the details of the previous night filled in: being picked up by the old man and driven to his high-up West End apartment.

I tossed back the sheets and crawled out of bed. At the window, I squinted through the venetian blinds against the glimmering waters of English Bay—almost noon, judging by the sun's height. Spied the last of yesterday's storm crowning the North Shore Mountains across the water.

At the foot of the bed were bright-white shelves overflowing with more books. I was downhearted at my ignorance, at how little I had accomplished in my life. I found my clothes stacked on the chair opposite me—dry, neatly folded, smelling of laundry detergent.

I dressed, then followed the sound of the typing to the living room. Seated at a small desk in front of the broad windows, Randall was reading whatever it was he had just written. He looked up and drew in a breath. "Aren't you a sight."

I must have looked awful with my bed-head and my ratty clothes hastily thrown on. I certainly felt terrible—hungover, red eyed, and achy, with a plugged-up nose. My face scrunched suddenly, then I let loose a sneeze.

"Sounds like that cold has settled in," he said. Scrutinizing again the page snugged against the carriage of the typewriter, he nodded toward the kitchen. "There's juice in the fridge. Hit the button on the coffee maker for a fresh brew. I'll make us breakfast in a minute. Just let me finish this." He scowled at the black lines hammered into the paper.

I hesitated to break his concentration or spoil the expansive scene through the big windows. "We didn't ... I mean, last night. Did we?"

"I told you, it's not like that. Besides," he said, raising his left hand so that the ring glinted in the sun pouring over the inlet. "I'm married."

Just then, there was a jostling of keys at the front door.

"And right on cue," he said.

A man wrestled his luggage through the opening and lowered it onto the marbled entranceway floor. He was short, mid-thirties probably, Asian, with a lean, friendly face, looking tired now from his long travels—judging by the two large suitcases. He shot me a quick smile as he crossed the living room, then gave Randall a peck on the lips.

"Another one of your strays, sweetheart?" The man tilted his head in my direction.

"Ted," Randall said, "I'd like you to meet my husband, Raymond. Raymond Takahashi."

As it turned out over the following months, I wasn't so much Randall's stray as Ray's. After he learned of my interest in art, Ray invited me to gallery openings, as well as the museum for a French Impressionists exhibition and another on Canada's own Group of Seven. Sunday mornings I'd often have breakfast at their apartment, all of North Van splayed out through the big picture windows. Afterward, Ray and I would take our sketch pads and walk to Stanley Park. We'd sit in the sun, or at the sheltered picnic tables when it spritzed, and draw whatever we liked. In that way, I first learned about perspective, foreshortening, how the image seems to flip in a figure–ground grouping.

After seeing my enthusiasm for the work, Ray encouraged me to attend the art school where he taught. He even wrangled a couple of grants. Talked me up with Admissions since my application was supported only by the Stanley Park sketches, drawings of birds snipped from my childhood notebooks, and his belief in the way I perceive the world as an interplay of form and colour.

One afternoon in their apartment, Ray and Randall's kindness finally overwhelmed me. These two men, so confident and accomplished, yet shadowed by old hurts. Boyhood bullies, hostile power brokers—blackballing Ray from gallery representation, terminating Randall's downtown investment house career—and shunning by family and friends.

And yet through their love, they had created another family—their many friends and new colleagues, Randall's collection of promising young men. That they included me in all this marked a reprieve, finally, from my detachment, my consignment to the depths. It was a feeling I'd not experienced since those ecstatic early days stomping around the mountains with Wade. My sadness over that loss and the loneliness I'd experienced afterward merged with my gratitude for the life my new friends had gifted me.

Curled on their couch, I began to bawl.

They sat alongside me and cradled the length of my body in their laps, stroking my face, my hair, my hands, as brothers might, had I had them. They called me darling.

all we have

I SNAPPED A new drawing pad onto the stand with two metal clips as the other art students filtered into the studio—through a forest of antique easels, past the glossy anatomical illustrations, the reproductions of life drawings by the Old Masters. A grey Vancouver morning, January 1961. The chill at my back poured through tall double-sash windows, the view through them halved by a fire escape along the diagonal.

Raymond Takahashi appeared in the doorway, his artist smock smudged with oil paint and acrylics. At the head of the room in front of a wide blackboard, he perched on the edge of a small desk and surveyed the class. He gave me the slightest of nods, and I echoed his discretion. We kept it businesslike at school, me only going as far as calling him Mr. T—like some of the other younger students. Never Ray, as I did at drunken house parties at his and Randall's apartment or when the three of us socialized there together.

The class was waiting on a young man new to posing that Ray had recently hired, who was undressing behind a privacy screen. The inked brushwork on the screen's dirty white silk was in a traditional Chinese theme—a landscape with a lone traveller at its centre dwarfed by the crags of a surrounding mountain scene.

That moment before the frenzied sketching began was my favourite time of day. The silence was a welcome retreat from the twists and turns life kept throwing at me. I studied my classmates, the light through the double-sash windows shadowing one side of their faces. Most of them appeared to be in their late teens to mid-twenties, recently out of high school like myself.

A few gave the impression they had kicked around quite a bit and had been kicked around in turn. While sketching, they appeared more animated than the young people in the room. Their faces cycled through excitement, wonder, disappointment, even disdain. Their shoulders slumped finally, they bowed to the familiar defeat by art, by age.

The model slipped out from behind the partition, wearing house slippers and a tattered blue bathrobe; he appeared to be my age, nineteen. Handsome, but in an unconventional way—his forehead too prominent under the short brown hair, his ears too large.

Ray tapped his fingers on the desktop. "All right, three-minute gestures."

He motioned with an open palm to the dais in the centre of the room, space heaters like the huts of sentinels emitting a rosy glow in two corners. The model mounted the platform. The thin robe puddled at his feet. Students reached for Conté and charcoal, flipped sheets in sketch pads. After Ray called "*begin*," the silence in the room was broken only by the scratch of crayons on paper, the occasional scrape of an easel on the concrete floor, or Ray's hushed comments as he circulated among the students.

The model was clad only in a white jockstrap. His physique was finely muscled, as that of a dancer or distance runner. In those short poses, he was a conjuror of dramatic gestures—arms outstretched to some longed-for horizon, or in a crouch as if weighed down by a tremendous burden. Accompanying these postures, expressions flickered across his face—now wide-eyed and open, now profoundly cruel, now vulnerable—each one jolting a spark through my body.

Since meeting Ray and Randall, I'd tried to fan that spark into a flame. The first time by accident, stumbling upon a washroom in Stanley Park, the smell of piss in my nostrils, getting drawn into a stall by some man I barely glimpsed. After returning to the scene of the crime for a couple more pitiful blow jobs, I went back to whacking off to my muscle mags.

My new friends scolded me for squandering my youth—Ray telling me, "Look at yourself in the mirror, darling. You can have anyone you want." They trotted out for my approval a parade of willowy, immaculately dressed, perfectly coiffed young men.

As difficult as my friendship with Wade had been, it was my touchstone. And though I concealed the kernel of myself from him, I felt we brought to each other not the masks that shielded us from the hostile, uncomprehending world of high school but our true faces.

That was so unlike the artifice of the candidates Ray and Randall presented me. You could sense despair in the way they held their cocktails, as if cradling Fabergé eggs in manicured hands. I wanted to be moved again by someone, and none of them moved me.

I felt something similar in the older models Ray hired for the class. With sagging, blemished bodies, bored and awkward, they ranged through unexpressive poses. I pictured myself the dispassionate surgeon scrutinizing a patient on an operating table—

as if they were mere contour and mass, muscle and ligament, dissected by my eye and hand.

I was taken aback, though, by this new model's urgency and perceived, as he hastened through the short poses, not so much craft as the expression of the native grace I craved. I was undone. Immobilized by his ferociousness, his oddball beauty. My hands hovered over the drawing pad, unable to contact its rough paper.

Ray startled me from my inertia, announcing the first twenty-minute sketch. The model struck a three-quarter back pose: Standing erect but relaxed, his weight shifted to his left leg, hand resting on that hip, the right leg held loosely in front of him and slightly bent.

Suddenly I was furiously slashing the Conté across the sheet, as if marking a line not on the paper but down the model's body itself. Stroking its muscles through the crayon—witnessing them for the first time. I experienced a kind of detachment I'd never known. As if there were no difference between the young man and me.

During the short poses, his eyes had been closed, which provided me with a bit of cover—not wanting him to be aware of my agitation. Whenever I glanced up during that long pose to check, say, how light shadowed his trapezius, I found him looking straight at me, holding my gaze, then slightly raising one eyebrow and shutting his eyes again. Which disconcerted me even more. And, though it interrupted my flow, I was relieved when Ray declared the fifteen-minute break.

Students set aside their drawing instruments and headed out the door for coffee at the café across the street. The model stretched, wrapped himself in his robe, extracted a bright-red apple from its pocket, and stepped down from the dais. As he munched on the fruit, he ambled around the room, examining drawings on easels or scattered on the floor.

I eyed my sketch, noting the clumsy foreshortening of the knee projected toward me.

A tap on my shoulder.

"You going for coffee?"

I stepped around to find Suzy, the girl who, for the past few months, I was supposedly dating. We had not yet kissed and had barely touched, which triggered both a huge sense of relief and a stubborn remorse.

She was dressed in a puffy grey turtleneck sweater, her black leotards showing off her trim legs. With her short hair, black eyeliner, and white lip gloss, she was doing her best Audrey Hepburn impersonation. She was a kick, that girl. As soon as the weather warmed, she would be out on the school's front steps, under the entrance's massive Egyptian-looking pylon, strumming a guitar and singing folk songs.

"No," I said, keeping an eye on the model, who was leafing through a stack of drawings on the floor. "Think I'll work a bit more on this last sketch."

Suzy sighed long and loudly, accompanying the performance with the rolling of her eyes. She presented her open palm, in which I placed a quarter fumbled from the pocket of my jeans. After she had gone, I erased the lower right leg on the sketch and from memory attempted to correct the foreshortening.

"Mind if I take a look?"

I started, nearly toppling my easel when the model spoke directly behind me.

"Yeah, sure," I said. "Though it's not very good yet."

He examined not the drawing on the easel but some older ones on the ripped pages at my feet. As he hunched down to get a better look, his robe pulled back to reveal his thighs. He crunched into the last of his apple, sat back on his heels. The movement parted the robe's fabric, opening a V from his shoulder, exposing a line of dark chest hair that dipped out of sight at his waist.

He paged unhurriedly through the sketches, resting finally on one of a model balancing on a leg, arm outstretched, torso torqued to the left. "Don't know how you get all that with so few lines."

"How do you come up with those crazy poses?"

He rose to his feet and looked me directly in the eyes. "No weak gestures. That's what Ray always says."

"Ray?"

"Yeah, you know. Takahashi."

"Aren't you new to modelling?"

"Here, yeah. But I've done some classes at UBC and some private sessions."

"Private?"

"Sure, that's how Ray and I met." He cinched the cord of his robe slightly. "Appears you've got a thing against declarative sentences."

"A what?"

The model chuckled, extended his hand. "Name's Paul."

I observed his fingers: slender, elegant. I lifted my own to match his greeting but noticed they were covered in red Conté. "My fingers, they're all ..."

"No worries," Paul said, slipping his right hand into mine and winking. "Not like I never got dirty before."

I clasped Paul's hand, cool from his standing so long in one position in that chilly room. I told him my name, feeling a little kick in my stomach as I noted the golden flecks in his irises.

He considered me a moment longer than I expected, then pivoted to examine my drawing clipped to the easel, the twenty-minute sketch capturing his features in the quickly drawn lines: his big ears, his upturned nose. He glanced from the drawing back to me, his head slightly cocked, and pinched the bridge of his nose. He raked a thumb outward along the skin below his eye, smudging a ruddy stripe across his cheekbone. "You sure got me there. Got me good. It's like looking in a mirror."

The classroom door burst open, students coursing in from their break.

"Back to the drawing board, eh?" Paul said, uncinching the cord at his waist to allow the hems of the robe to drape apart.

My eyes darted from his jockstrap to Suzy standing just inside the doorway watching us, a paper coffee cup in each hand. I stepped backward, away from Paul, unable to prevent the blush from rising in my face.

"You ..." I stammered as he turned toward the dais. "You've got Conté smudged across your cheek."

Paul regarded the smear of chalk in his right palm, ground his thumb into it. He reached forward and drew the rusty red across my skin, outlining my eye socket's lower ridge.

"There," he said. "We're like brothers now."

—

I sprinted up the stairs to the third-floor walk-up that served as Ray's studio. The thick cardboard of the drawing pad chafed my armpit through my winter coat. I barely noticed it; I was so excited over my tête-à-tête moments earlier with Paul in life-drawing class. His behaviour felt flirtatious, which Ray confirmed when I interrogated him after the schoolroom had emptied.

Ray cast a quick look at the blur of students in the hallway rushing to the next session and told me some men behave like that. The hot ones, especially. It was their way of establishing authority. He wouldn't reveal Paul's sexuality, reminding me people kept that under wraps. He hinted, though, that at the private sessions he arranged for his gay artist friends—for whom Paul modelled—the young man appeared completely at home.

I turned my key in the lock and shouldered the wooden door, its sticky hinges at last giving way. When it burst open—my clumsy arms and legs doing a flat-footed dance—I lurched into the narrow room.

On the back wall, a grid of small-paned windows opened to the North Shore Mountains, whose slopes were basted with tatters of white clouds beneath a mantle of grey stratus. Another cold front, perhaps, descending from the northwest.

From a skylight—the glass's cross-hatched chicken wire obscured in the accumulated grime—a diffuse luminosity poured onto raw canvases slabbed against the side walls. Hung salon-style above them were fifteen or so completed pieces. Their riot of swooping, mostly colourless forms—like Japanese brushwork—echoed Ray's abstract-expressionist heroes.

Crowded into one corner was a table with my paints and palettes, an easel I'd repaired—one of the school's originals from the '20s, judging by the rough state in which I'd found it.

My pack thudded onto the threadbare couch where I sometimes slept when I worked too late and missed the last bus, where I meant to bunk that night. I perched the sketch pad across the arms of a shabby upholstered chair and slipped out the drawings I had just completed.

I had handed in three of the best as Ray requested. Seated at his desk in the classroom, he'd examined them one by one in the light flooding through the tall windows. His pleasure at viewing my sketches was always obvious, something he masked when among the other students, not wishing to be caught playing favourites. Ray was particularly pleased that day, he told me. It was the first he'd witnessed me transcend the merely technical and capture some real feelings.

I'd withheld from him the sketch of the sustained twenty-minute pose. The standing three-quarter back view with the foreshortened leg that needed correcting. I was still shaken by what occurred during that pose, never having experienced such a loss of control. It frightened me, the cruelty embedded in Paul's gesture, the determined look on his face, almost a sneer.

It excited me as well. I told myself I would make the sketch the basis of a painting—starting that afternoon with some studies on paper—but I knew why I really kept it.

Lowering the drawing to the floor, kneeling in front of it, I perceived its power emanating off the light-grey sheet, the sexual suggested by the slightly cocked hip, the non-supporting leg loosely turned out so the fleshiness of Paul's thigh was presented to me. Reaching out to the page, I traced its outline, my finger smudging the crayon.

My old habit of fantasizing overcame me in a fabrication I now think of as prescient, having dreamed of something similar with other men—though never quite so poetically. I pictured Paul and me in our bed in a house we built on a lake somewhere in the mountains near Harrison. There were days, long stretches when we only rose from the sheets to piss or to forage in the kitchen between bouts of sex or sleeping, curled in each other's limbs, soothed by the rippling of water outside our windows. There too was a loosening of self so that alongside Paul and me was the presence of a third—not either of us but both at once. That awareness cocooned us in our bed, for in it was a sensation of repair. The wounds accumulated over our short lives scabbing and peeling off to reveal the bright-pink skin of *us*.

Pain in my knees intruded. The mountains on the opposite shore of Burrard Inlet were rouged by the setting sun. How much time had I spent, lost there, imagining my real life to come?

I scrambled to a standing position, hobbled to the couch. Sprawling upon it, resting my head on my pack, my hand drifted down my torso, loosened my belt, fingers slipping under the waistband.

—

I pulled the cord on the bus before reaching school, a full three stops away. Admin had cancelled Thursday's classes for an instructor something or other, and I was keyed up over having waited a week to see Paul. I wanted that magic again, the interplay between hand and eye, scrutinizing every detail shadowed across his nearly naked body and translating it onto the page.

More than anything, though, I needed to talk to him. Over the last few days, our imaginary life in our lakeside love nest had lost its intensity. Since I knew so little about him, I lacked the specifics to power my fairy tale. How the folds of the pillow marked his face when he first woke, the way he held his coffee cup at breakfast, the little things that made him happy, that pissed him off.

That morning, the weather was glorious, the sky washed by the previous evening's storm into the brightest blue. I sprinted the five blocks to class, attempting to tamp down my excitement so as not to appear the sappy romantic when I saw Paul. Rounding the corner of our school, I found him leaning against one of the abstract alabaster salmon at the foot of the stairs. The monumental entrance facade towered over him, its faux-hieroglyphic flora and fauna incised into the grey concrete.

"Hey," Paul said, a smile spreading from ear to ear.

I was dumbstruck, as bewitched as I'd been the first time I saw him.

"You okay?"

Paul reached over, cupping his hand around my forearm, and I jolted as if suddenly shaken awake.

"I got my wires crossed today," he said. "Forgot Ray hired that old lady model. The one with the saggy bazookas."

Suzy brushed past me and hurried up the stairs, glancing back at Paul and me when she reached the top landing.

"Was thinking," Paul said, "it's too pretty to be inside. Why don't you skip class? Maybe the two of us could take a walk." He ran a thumb along the ridgeline under his right eye. "You know, brother to brother."

At that callback, another jolt—an electric sensation coursing up my spine, my mind quieting. Though I still hadn't managed to say a word, I must have signalled my agreement for I found myself following him around the corner to Victory Square, the Dominion Building's vermilion top aglow in the afternoon sun. Heading west, we passed the steam clock, the stately white columns of Waterfront Station. On its port side, we dashed through the tidal flats, the snowy peak of Grouse Mountain smiling at us from across the harbour. I noted the animal good nature with which Paul threaded his way down the muddy shoal and bounded over shallow pools.

That same fierceness of purpose had so compelled me with Wade—the intensity of his actions, his desires. And mirroring him striding down our boyhood spawning grounds was Paul as he leapt along the harbour's edge.

I understood at last that their physical beauty—which for so long had thrilled and oppressed me—was only a costume. Something that both hid and revealed the thing below I craved: the essence of these men that I struggled to capture on the page.

On a rocky shoal edging the harbour, we spread our coats and sat, the sun warming us through our sweaters. I thought again of the fantastical versions of ourselves lovestruck at our cabin and was saddened by how far we were from that kind of connection. I struggled for some way to bridge the gap. "I don't see how you stay so still—in the long poses," I said, retreading ground.

"Weight-bearing gestures, no outstretched arms. Let your bones do the work."

"I guess I mean mentally, with everyone staring."

"I don't mind being looked at," Paul said, a slight breeze luffing his brown hair. "With some people, I quite like it." He directed his smile to me, searching my eyes for a moment, then glancing away. "And it gives me time to think about what I'm doing with my life."

What he was doing, he said, was taking a year off after high school, grubstaked by his father, a prosperous Winnipeg businessman. The posing thing was for fun, a way to meet interesting people—something he told me he could never do in Winnipeg. Appearing pained for a moment, he surveyed the length of the harbour.

I outlined my particulars, not that there was much to report. Our family's clapboard bungalow, our small hometown. My dotty mom out in her garden reciting Romantic poetry. My dad in the village pool singing songs of his homeland—"The Rose of Tralee," "The Irish Rover"—his whole body stretched out on the surface, supported by the warm water of the hot springs.

Paul hurled a rock into the choppy harbour, and the distressed expression again washed across his face, then was gone. In the silence that followed, I sensed a shift take place between us, some rough correspondence over our small-town childhoods, our loving, if somewhat tiresome, families.

At last, his features morphed into a toothy smile, and he said, "You feel like coming over Friday night? My housemates and I are throwing a big party."

—

As kids jostled past, I clung to a newel post for dear life, winded from elbowing through the crowd up three floors—past peeling wallpaper, yellowed and water stained with age—to the top of the oval staircase in a rambling old house near UBC.

When I finally reached what they called "Paul's Pad"—a closet, really, off a dark hall in the former servants' quarters—I found it crammed with people huddled under a cloud of tobacco and marijuana smoke. Paul leapt up when he caught sight of me, tumbled over the rows of outstretched legs, and fell into my arms.

The side of Paul's face nuzzled my cheek as he shouted in my ear over the music. "Stay right here. I'll get us some beers. Oh man. It's so good to see you. I wasn't sure you'd come."

I hadn't been certain myself. I had promised Suzy I'd take her to *La Dolce Vita* at the Majestic and planned to call it an early night afterward in order to make the 8 a.m. bus to Harrison for a weekend with my parents. Though I knew Suzy to be a Fellini freak, when I broke the news to her about not being able to make it Friday night, she didn't seem especially disappointed.

Paul tripped coming up the stairs from the second-floor landing, beer from brown bottles foaming a dark spot on his jeans. "Oh man." He offered me one of the half-empty brews, then placed me in a bear hug. "Oh man, it's so great. You came. I'm so glad."

He was talking fast, his head swivelling to take in each passerby. When he focused again on me, I noticed his pupils were dilated.

"I'm so fucked up," he said. "Come on, let's check out the dancing."

Paul started down the oval staircase again, grabbing my hand and pulling me after him. At his touch, a wave of lust, affection, and a fierce loyalty swept through me. At the same time, I experienced an urge to jerk my hand away, though none of the kids lounging on the steps, talking, paid us any mind.

We fairly skipped down the stairs toward the thumping bass and brass, Chubby Checker crooning "The Twist" over the doo-wop backup singers. In the living room, the few pieces of furniture were shoved to the periphery, and in the low ruddy light kids swung their arms and legs side to side in the dance that had been such a craze. As we hit the bottom step, a girl with long black hair and flaring Cleopatra eyeliner yelled Paul's name, pressed through the dancers, and threw her arms around him.

"Where you been?" she said. "You disappeared ages ago. You promised me a dance." She pulled him into the living room. He jumped about, crashing into nearby couples and launching one kid forward, whose drink erupted from a plastic cup to drench some poor girl in a leather halter top.

Cleopatra hauled Paul away from more disasters and dumped him in front of me. "Here," she said, "he's all yours. Friggin' psycho." She pecked him on the forehead, then made her way to the kitchen, gabbing to a girl who wore a pink tutu and a Mickey Mouse Club hat.

I propped myself against the wall, sipping my beer. Having lost his, Paul held a hand up to the red light bulbs in the ceiling fixture, wiggling his fingers. The young people gyrating in front of us appeared as if they were a single organism, expanding and contracting—each individual swallowed in the life of the whole. The sight of this sweaty, smiling mass moving as one to the music made me feel even more the outlier. I stashed my beer and was about to shrink off into some dark corner and light a cigarette when Paul seized my hand again.

"Let's dance. Come on. I promise to be a good boy."

I froze, wrenched my hand away. "But I don't have anybody to ..."

Paul leaned in so that as he spoke his breath fluttered across the side of my face. "It's okay, Ted. It's not like that anymore. You can dance with yourself. Or everyone." He squeezed my hand and winked. "You can even dance with *me*."

Laughing, he placed his hands on my shoulders and steered us into the crush of swaying partygoers. A new forty-five dropped on the record player, and, after a scratchy pause, the Marvelettes harmonized "Please Mr. Postman." Dancing was something I'd never done well, but I began loosening up, swinging back and forth with the others to the girl group's jaunty song.

His eyes closed, Paul raised his arms, weaving his hands together in a soaring dance all of their own. In the room—hot now, womblike with the red light pouring down—Paul's movements were those of an exotic animal, some prince schooled in seduction. As his sweater drifted downward to reveal his muscular arms, I could barely stop myself from running into them. I inclined forward, holding his gaze as his eyes searched my face.

Someone gave me a joint, and I passed it on without toking up. I experienced a rush of happiness even so. In the muddle of bumping and grinding, Paul was turning more and more to nudge me with his hips. Beaming at me, mouthing the song's lyrics.

Some guys lurking at the edge of the dancers called his name, reaching over to shake his hand. A few girls rushed in, framed his face in their fingers, and peppered him with kisses. They spun him around, and he was swallowed in the crowd.

Suddenly another kid was bopping in front of me. He grinned widely, sashayed close to cup his hands around my waist. I pushed him away and lurched back. My eyes swept the dance floor for Paul, then skidded to a stop on Suzy across the room dancing with another girl.

Just then the music slowed: the tinkling chords of Patsy Cline's "Crazy." People paired off—even two guys dancing together. And Suzy, she was folded in that girl's arms, snogging her openly in the dim red light.

Something inside me short-circuited: an electrical chittering up my spine.

Without thinking, I bolted.

Clawing like a junkyard dog through coats piled in a bedroom. Crushed by the crowd, plunging into the hallway. There Paul—a beer in each hand—jabbered to a couple of girls in tennis outfits, both flushed as if straight off the court. While I was swept outside by people rushing to light up cigarettes on the sidewalk.

Why was I suddenly sprinting from what I'd always dreamed of?

Those young guys dancing together.

And Suzy kissing the girl, that should have been a relief. We could finally drop the charade of dating.

Paul shouted my name through the open front door. But I was halfway down the block, ramming my arms into my jacket.

Running where?

To Joanne's off-campus apartment. Only three blocks. I badly needed her schooling me on what an idiot I was, then bucking me up.

But no—she and her new grad school pals were out of town for the weekend. For some literary gathering.

So I headed to the beach. Just down those twisty residential streets: English Bay.

There, the sound of waves rode the incoming tide. I collapsed on a patch of grass on the narrow shoreline, kicked off my tennis shoes, and peeled off my socks. I sank my toes into the sand, both braced and repelled by its clamminess. Lights from a cargo ship hulking in the shadows smeared a red line across the dark water. Electric sensations again sparked up my spine, as they had moments earlier on the dance floor.

Suddenly I was fourteen. Leaden limbed, downstream from that log boom, sinking beneath the cold surface of the river. How beautiful the fingers of sunlight there, the shimmering bright-green curtain they made. That beauty diverted me from the struggle to hold my breath. As troubling as the struggle became, even more so was what seemed to lurk below in the darkness.

Though I grasped it dimly that night, as lights rippled on the waters of the bay, I see clearly now what finally carried me to safety. It wasn't that danger lurking below that sparked the pulse through my limbs but the depth of my longing for it.

At the sound of running shoes striking the pavement, this half-formed understanding dissolved.

It was Paul—panting, wrestling into his winter coat.

"What the fuck?" he said. "Why'd you run away, Ted? We were having fun."

I was speechless, my thoughts still in shambles. Shaking from the cold, I crammed my feet back into my shoes, zipped up my coat, and gripped it at the collar.

Paul shrugged out of his jacket and draped it across my shoulders, even though it left him in only a light sweater. Lowering himself beside me, he hugged his chest and scanned the dark water. This time not in a stoner's awe, I sensed, but as if weighing his words before speaking. After some moments, he began, almost in a murmur, muffled by the pulsing surf.

"I lied to you," he said.

"Oh? About what?"

"I'm not in Vancouver taking a year off from school, bankrolled by my family. I don't have a family anymore."

He told me he had only one memory of his mother, when he was three or so, shortly before she died. Just a face hovering above him, an accompanying feeling of wholeness and well-being.

Last summer, he said, when he was eighteen, he lost his father too.

Because Paul had attempted to kiss another boy. Before the lips touched, though, both he and his friend recoiled. Paul, since he understood he was breaking the rule that for so long had kept his world from teetering off the rails. His friend, considering the sour expression on his face, because of disgust.

A week later, ditching his bike in the yard, Paul came upon his friend's father red faced and gesturing wildly. A Monsanto exec, he was a mover and shaker around town—a sharp dresser and known for being a bully. Paul's soft-spoken father, a shop owner prone to go along to get along, withered that day under the man's finger pointing.

Paul told me his father wasn't religious, just unable to tolerate mess. After apologizing for being a single parent who, on account of business, was "insufficiently engaged," Paul's father concluded all his son needed was a "firm hand." Military school was "deemed in order." If Paul truly had proclivities—his father wasn't convinced based on that single incident—"discipline and rigour would surely amend them."

Paul couldn't stand it when his father spoke this way, like he was lecturing some deadbeat customer behind on his payments. In a fuck-you before being shipped off, Paul cleaned out the petty cash at his father's hardware store. Then he fished in his pocket, found a quarter, and flipped it. Heads. He was going west.

His bus ticket, though, only got him as far as Calgary. Collect calls and grovelling didn't appease his father, who declined to fund Paul's return to Winnipeg. Three words—"discipline and rigour"—were all his father offered.

In front of us, a tug rumbled toward the narrows, tossing its wake onto the sand. At the prow, a lone sailor scanning for deadheads swept a searchlight across the water. I shivered in the chill air as the beam raked over Paul's troubled face.

"Fuck," I said. "How could your old man do that?"

"In a weird way, he was right. I mean it's messed up, but I'm figuring it out."

Paul recounted how he was hired as a dishwasher at the bus station's diner. The manager let him crash in the back, and the first night blew Paul for five dollars cash. After a month of that, plus giving the fat slob head and sometimes taking it up the ass, Paul banked enough to continue his western journey.

Paul told me it was a trip when his train made it to the station in Vancouver and he stepped onto the platform—into the mild, salty air. So different from the hot, high-plains dryness of summers in Winnipeg.

There, Paul had shelled out fifteen dollars for a fake ID that didn't fool anybody. He was freaked the cops would bust him back to his dad, and work was hard to come by, always temporary. With a shovel or wheelbarrow, boxes stacked in warehouses, or dishes piled sky high in restaurant sinks.

When he couldn't even afford the windowless, tobacco-stinking flophouse under the Granville Bridge, Paul ran with a pack of street kids who scrambled into the cars of random guys. For a twenty, they hauled Paul somewhere sketchy; he gave them head, then got dumped back on the street. Or he bottomed in some john's place out in the burbs and spent hours hitching his way back.

As he related this, I felt a rush of concern and embarrassment. Envy, even, because of having been with so few men myself.

"It wasn't all bad. It got me off the streets. I started working the bars, met some nice men. Older men."

"Ray and Randall?" I said, again experiencing the mix of moral squeamishness and jealousy, this time over him being more intimate than I with my friends.

"No. Well, Randall, but only the once. Mostly, I was another of his strays. Like you, I guess. They got me out of hustling, found that place back there with some of Randall's students. And my job. I'm still taking off my clothes, but it's not the same."

"What about your father?"

"Haven't spoken to him in a year. Fuck him. I'm never going back to that shithole Winnipeg."

Thinking back now to the fathers of previous generations—Paul's, Wade's, Wade's maternal grandfather—they were all men who skulked on the periphery of their families, strangers who passed their unhappiness onto their children. My own father, as I picture him now, was a pugnacious Dubliner as a lad, enjoying fisticuffs and tall tales told over a pint. Middle age tempered him. He became soft spoken, drifting on waves of lilting, Irish-inflected words, none of them used to express how he felt. Even so, he wore his emotions on his sleeve, often embracing Mother and me, his tears flowing readily—as do mine.

Paul began to shudder with the cold, his breath hitching and emitting mist that swirled about his face. I returned his coat. "Why are you telling me all this?"

"You're kind of quiet. A good listener, I guess. A little sad too." He shimmied into the jacket, picked up a stick, scratched a smiley face in the sand. "And I don't have anyone to talk to, really."

"Looks to me like everybody loves you." I gestured over my shoulder in the direction of the house party.

"Oh, that," he said. "It's just for show."

It was thrilling, his confiding in me—a step toward the romance I fantasized. With it, though, came an insecurity, a fear of rejection—something new I had to be willing to risk.

"And now what are you going to do?" I said, attempting to sound more assured than I felt.

"I'm saving up for my education. Randall says he can get me a scholarship in his department. Business, that's what I'm thinking. Something practical, since I'm having to make it on my own."

He threaded a pack of cigarettes out of a coat pocket and jostled out a hand-rolled joint. Its ends twisted into tight tips like withered white blossoms.

"I never ..." I said, shaking my head.

"Go on, you'll like it."

He struck a wooden match on his jeans, and I toked up, attempting not to act like the novice, suppressing a cough. I was dizzy and elated, feeling as if we were inching even further toward that love I craved.

"You still high?" I said.

"Completely baked."

"Maybe you shouldn't, then." I licked my fingers and was about to pinch out the joint.

"Oh no you don't. Hand that over, mister. Tonight, we're celebrating."

"Celebrating what?"

He seized my coat collar and tugged me toward him, his face looming suddenly out of the dark. Lips locking onto mine, he was sucking my tongue into his mouth, then biting my lips. He forced me backward onto the sand, hauled my hands above my head, clasped them by the wrists while grinding his hips into mine.

I twisted my head sideways to catch a breath. On the deck of that nearby cargo ship, fireflies bobbed up and down: crew members smoking cigarettes. The image of Paul and me at that lake house flashed in my mind. Our bed, where we sometimes argued but were never really out of sync. Our lovemaking and tears. Naked, pressing into each other, straining ever closer in the advancing morning light.

"Stop," I said, forcing Paul off me and sidling out from under him. "Slow down. I'm not one of your tricks."

Paul pushed onto all fours and, crab-like, scrambled away a short distance. Though I couldn't see his face, the hurt and anger in his voice were unmistakable. "What the fuck, Ted? I just poured my guts out. Think I feel good about this? Nobody knows except Ray and Randall. I told you because I thought we were becoming friends."

"We are … I just … You're wasted, Paul. I don't want … Not like this."

"This is exactly what you want," he said, his voice a low growl, thick with desire. Reaching over, he cupped my cock. It was painfully hard, straining against the dark-blue cloth of my jeans. My eyes closed, my shoulders slackened, and I let out a sigh.

At once, he stripped off his coat and pounced on me again. His mouth bore down on mine, hands ripping off my jacket, jerking my sweater over my head, fingers blundering with the buttons of my shirt. His tongue darted into my ear, and a cascade of tremors guttered down my back.

A line of kids filed down the trail behind us, heading for the surf. They were laughing loudly while passing around a small pipe.

I pushed Paul away.

"Come on," he said. His voice sounded so childlike I began to relent. I understood even then that behind this rough behaviour were our hormones, the urgency of being nineteen. And behind the desperate craving, I sensed his need for relief from the hurt life dealt him—for a moment's connection to make up for what he had lost.

"I just want to get my rocks off," he said.

At this, all sympathy for him vanished. His tricks queued up before me—him fucking them, getting fucked by them, an empty lust propelling the thing. And then the embarrassment afterward—one I would go on to feel often—at having been caught so unguarded and raw. But that night the image turned me on. My noble aspirations melted under his kisses. They drained, like the useless things they were, into the sand.

"Okay," I said, "but not here."

"My room, then."

"It's probably full of passed-out kids."

"Your place." He murmured in my ear.

"The landlady watches us like a hawk. Visitors are against the rules."

"Fuck the rules." He was pawing open my shirt now, his fingernails scratching red lines down my chest.

I thought of Ray. His studio. Friday nights, though, he was usually there painting. But I needed this. I so needed this.

The stoners on the beach were belting some high-spirited melody while skipping hand in hand down the hardpacked sand between us and the water.

One of them interrupted her singing to scowl over at Paul and me grappling in the weeds. "Jeez, morons," she said, "get a fucking room."

Startled, Paul tumbled off me onto his side. I scrambled out from under him and sprang to my feet. "Beat it!" I shouted at the girl. Her face mocking a churlish ten-year-old's, she curtsied, then scurried back to the singers.

I returned my attention to Paul, who was seated, his eyes fixed on the lights of the cargo ship across the bay.

"Look, let's wait," I said. "When you're not so loaded. When we know each other a little better. We don't have to do this now."

"All we have is now, Ted," Paul said, struggling back into his coat, his voice sad, no longer pleading.

—

I caught the bus Saturday, as planned, only to find when I arrived in Harrison that Mom had broken her foot and had checked into the hospital. She was in there two days, then peg-legged and incapacitated at the house. Since Dad had to work at the resort, I stayed on for a week to look after her.

I phoned Ray and asked him to let Paul know that I'd been delayed, that I wanted to straighten things out. Ray seemed guarded, saying he couldn't talk, and quickly cut off the call.

Upon returning from Harrison, I raced up the art school's front steps, under the panel of fake glyphs. I found Ray stationed behind his desk in his otherwise empty classroom while from behind the partition came the rustling of clothes as Paul undressed.

"Look, I'm sorry about what happened after the party." I figured there was no need to be cagey around Ray, who had probably already gotten an earful.

"Ted," Ray said.

"It's all so new to me, Paul. But I'm in. Whatever you want."

Ray jolted to his feet, thrusting back his chair, the metal glides squealing on the concrete. "Ted, please. That's enough."

From around the corner of the privacy screen stepped the old woman Ray sometimes employed, her breasts ballooning the fluffy blue bathrobe.

"Paul is in Whistler, Ted," Ray said. "Working at a ski resort for the rest of the season."

My face burned, flushing with annoyance. "You knew this when I called last week?"

"I wasn't sure. And I didn't think it was my place to tell you."

"You're practically my only friend, Ray. Whose place would it be?"

The model squinted and scowled. From the robe's pocket, she retrieved the portable radio she sometimes listened to during long poses, plugged in her earphones, and sequestered herself behind the screen.

"I'm sorry," Ray said. "I just thought ... He's a free spirit, Ted. You knew that." He peered first at the privacy screen, then at the students streaming past the open doorway.

His discomfort gave me a beat of pleasure, which—as he stood there, fretting—suddenly amped to full-bore anger. "All those fags you turn me on to, but you never introduced me to him?"

"Please keep your voice down, Ted."

And though his overly cautious nature irked me, what annoyed me even more was his aversion to conflict. I'd never known him to stand up to anyone, especially when he should—say, with Randall's strays, who sometimes leveraged youth and beauty to their advantage.

"I was protecting you," he said.

My anger then utterly gave way. My puffed-up romantic notions had managed to stereotype me, and Ray's mothering—ordinarily so touching—now seemed a reproach for my failings.

I crumpled onto a stool behind one of the easels, letting my drawing pad drop to the floor. Slumping forward, I buried my head in my palms, ashamed at having allowed my pettiness to spoil my affection for my friend.

Ray crossed the room to stand beside me, his hand hovering mid-air for a moment before lighting on my shoulder. "You'll get over this, darling. We all have."

In my mind, I glimpsed the love nest on the lake near Harrison. It was collapsing onto itself, bursting into flame. I viewed its blackened and burnt-out shell.

"Look, here's the plan," Ray said, giving my shoulder a squeeze. "No arguments. You'll come to dinner tonight. We three will have a good cry. God knows there's plenty to cry about. We'll knock back Randall's pricey Cabernet, get plastered, and howl at the moon. If it's not out, we'll use our imaginations. We have that. Don't we, darling?"

I lifted my hand across my chest and rested it on his, before Ray withdrew and returned to his desk.

Now, I feel myself merging once more into that moment: the light streaming from the tall windows, the forest of listing, paint-splattered easels. I hear my Keds slap the concrete as I hop from the stool to retrieve my pad. Had I been more objective then, I might have understood I'd reached an adult milestone—the loss of first love. Glad it would remain in this soft glow of memory.

Then, though, sad and slightly numbed, I clipped the drawing pad to the easel. And, slipping from my pack the plastic case of Conté crayons, I let out a sigh, then waited for Suzy and the rest of my classmates to troop in.

before the revolution

ANXIOUS TO ESCAPE the drizzle and cold, I stashed my VW Beetle on Hastings and—shoulders hunched, collar up—hustled along the rain-slicked sidewalk. In the entryway of an abandoned building, a sleeper in a cardboard sarcophagus. Sheltered under a tattered awning, hookers eyeing me hungrily. And blundering into me, a haggard fellow transfixed by the neon in the barred window of a pawnshop.

January 1964. Downtown Eastside, Vancouver.

That wasn't exactly the place I wanted to spend my Saturday night. But it was there I found the Montreal Club—the biggest gay bar in town—where I could dance, have a good time, and, with any luck, meet someone.

That possibility had lured me through those bleak surroundings for three years. Since I ditched the ingenue routine and its insipid romantic fantasies, I'd been making discoveries and mistakes, making up for lost time. One-night stands, next morning hangovers—I suffered them willingly, took pride, even, in my worldly nonchalance.

Before ducking off Hastings, I caught a glimpse of the Smilin' Buddha, a nightclub catering to rockers and wannabe hipsters slumming it Eastside. Its cheerful illuminated sign and prominent position on the strip, the boisterous punks smoking in the alcove out front, clashed with the nameless entranceway and the deserted, poorly lit stairwell I began to climb. I glanced repeatedly over my shoulder until I reached the top landing, then pressed a buzzer and waited.

Through the wall, laughter and voices over the blare of music.

In what resembled a theatre ticket booth, a woman slipped through a tattered velvet curtain. She appeared to be in her mid-forties, with a rumpled, expressionless face. Probably the mobbed-up manager's fresh squeeze.

At twenty-two—though I had finally lost my baby fat—I was sometimes mistaken as underage. So, even though the ID I slipped under the glass with my fiver was finally legit, I squirmed as she gave me the once-over. I must have made the grade, or her discomfort with yet another fag was too great, since she waved me off with one bejewelled hand.

As disconcerting as that gauntlet was, when the door buzzed and I pushed through into the bar, half the eyeballs there snapped to attention. Whenever that happened, I felt as if I were making an entrance in a stage play for which I was miscast and underprepared. Savour it, some of the older fellows counselled, but the sooner I melted into the crowd, the better I felt.

Illuminated by naked bulbs suspended from the ceiling, much of the narrow room was occupied by the dance floor, though a line of booths and tables hugged the long side walls. That night, the place was jammed, mostly with people I'd never seen—guys bopping with other guys, girls with girls. There were even a few straight couples in the mix, out at the gay bar to amp up their cool cred.

The place being unlicensed, I cached my flask in my jacket, which I pegged alongside a row of others in a dark corner—though not before taking a hefty swig.

"Ted!" Suzy shouted above the din. Her arms outstretched, she barged toward me through the crowd, towing behind her a butch girl in a flannel shirt and workboots. After Suzy's hugs and chaste kisses, red faced and talking fast she dragged me onto the floor.

While I was still an unfortunate dancer, I allowed myself to sway to the mid-tempo beat, inhaling deeply and closing my eyes while Mary Wells sang "My Guy" on the jukebox. When I resurfaced, I noticed the girls were moving more rapidly than the music warranted. My guess was my friend had been into her mother's diet pills again.

I gyrated close to yell at her over the music. "Who else did you come with?"

She pointed to Michael, another art student in my year. When I gave him a wave, his piercing blue eyes beneath too-perfect brows locked onto mine. Though dancing that night in ripped dungarees and a grey tank top that complemented his good looks, he was usually clothed with considerable flair. Even when he wore a collared shirt and jeans, the pants were pressed to a knife edge, the jersey tie-dyed or batiked, topped by a jaunty scarf. This, and the brilliance of his work, set him apart from the scruffiness and underdeveloped artistry of the other students, me included.

Behind Michael, through cigarette smoke the movements of one boy on the dance floor attracted my notice. He was eighteen, maybe nineteen. A sheen of sweat coated his face and arms. With his curly black hair, dark complexion, and white T-shirt, the young man could have jumped right out of *West Side Story*.

I waved to the girls, then plowed through the dancers to the snack bar at the far end of the room, where the hustlers hung out. As usual, Jim was there—chatting up a towheaded kid with ruined teeth and a pimply complexion.

Jim was around forty, a guy I tricked with once before I knew any better. A few bruises to my body and ego weren't all I came away with. I caught my first case of crabs. No surprise really, since his mission in life was to seduce every new and attractive young man who stole through the club door. So, I went to him for the lay of the land.

"Who's that?" I said, tilting my head in the direction of the dancing dark-haired boy.

"Don't know," Jim grumbled. "But whoever he is, he's not very friendly. Wouldn't waste your time."

Despite the warning, I couldn't take my eyes off the boy. His swooping arms and leaps and turns showed a real feel for the music. He wasn't merely plodding side to side—as I usually did—like those lacklustre dancers out on the floor. And though he appeared oblivious to everyone around him, he noticed me watching. He shot me a quick smile, shrugged, then continued his graceful inventions.

At the end of the song, the young man meandered through the crush of dancers to a booth where a pair of sour-faced Laurel and Hardy look-alikes had fixed their attention on him. As the three chatted, the skinny one eyed me warily while the plump fellow pawed the young man. Every so often, the boy glanced my way to see if I was still checking him out.

When he ambled to the snack bar and stood beside me, I plucked up my courage. "I've been watching you dance," I said.

He shot me a sexy grin while he rocked in half time to the beat. "It's great finally finding a place like this—though it's a total dump. I had no idea there were ..."

Someone dropped a quarter in the jukebox on a fast song: crashing cymbals and saxes, Little Richard blasting out "Keep a Knockin'."

I leaned forward, cupping a hand, and grazed his ear. "You've never been here before?"

"No." His hazel eyes darted over my face as I drew back.

"So where do you go?" I shouted.

"Most of the time I'm studying. I'm first-year biology at UBC. Keeps my nose to the grind, and me out of too much trouble."

"You get into trouble?" Smiling, I arched an eyebrow.

The boy grinned broadly, ignoring the throng milling about to focus on me. He resumed bopping to the song, and I bounced around with him. We danced apart but close. Bellowing above the music and conversation, I told him my name and asked for his. Marc, he said, spelled with a *c*—short for Marcus. His mom was Italian. Dad was the usual BC mix—Scots/Irish/English mongrel.

I observed the two men in the booth eyeballing us and asked if the heavyset guy was his boyfriend. Marc chuckled and told me he would sure like to be. Last summer, they had all worked at a sawmill near Kamloops, where the men resided. The two friends travelled to Vancouver some weekends to party, and earlier that evening they had rung Marc up and dragged him out.

"So here I am." He spread his arms wide as if to exclaim "ta-dah!"

"Well, Marc with a *c*, if you don't go out ..."

"I didn't say that!" he hollered. "I do get out but not overnight. I still live with my parents."

I tracked the way his body moved, how it rode the music. "Where do you go, then?"

"Places" was all he offered as Little Richard and the throaty sax faded out.

A slow number followed—Ray Charles crooning "That Lucky Old Sun." Smiles broadened across our faces, lighting up our eyes as we shifted to low gear. Hands fixed at our sides, we danced a few inches apart, resisting the magical field tugging us together, savouring the moment before the first spark when we finally touched. Pressing into one another, there was no hesitancy, no awkwardness over who was leading.

As our breathing slowed, my hand explored his back, running down the ridge of his spine to cup his ass. His lips brushed my neck, nibbled my ear, then drifted across my cheek to finally lock onto my mouth. We remained glommed onto each other, radiating heat, rocking back and forth, my leg pulsing between his thighs. Then my fingers snuck under his belt, between underwear and skin, to brush against the tip.

A sudden intake of breath.

"Fuck," he whispered in my ear, "I couldn't stop."

I held him tightly as the tremors subsided, then he told me he'd better clean up and headed to the washroom. Manoeuvring into the shadows, I lolled against a wall to revel in the lingering sensation of his body snugged against mine.

After a few moments Marc reappeared in the passageway that led to the washroom, his eyes searching the dance floor. His worried expression morphed into a grin, and he approached me. "I thought maybe you'd split."

I'd fretted over him doing the same. Smiling, I shook my head. "Not a chance."

He stared at his feet, then up along my slender frame. "What happened on the dance floor ..."

"Was exciting," I said. "Still is."

"Yes, I can see that." He beamed.

Just then, the buzzer blared. The ceiling lights flashed, then brightened, and the music cut off. Couples quickly disengaged, snugged contraband into crumpled paper sacks, which they hurriedly stashed behind trash receptacles in dark corners.

The room broke into a sort of manic fire drill, women swapping out with the odd man at the booths and tables. Men tag teaming with women to loiter in mixed company along the walls. I dragged Marc across the room and deposited him in front of Suzy, then rested my hands on the shoulders of her friend.

The air seemed to have deserted the room as everyone eyed the cops barging in. There were two males, along with a female officer who was charged with inspecting the butches' waistbands for offending masculine underwear.

I worried one of the men would ID Marc because he appeared so young, but Suzy had the presence of mind to deliver him a smackingly amorous kiss just as the officer approached. He prodded them apart with his nightstick, then continued, along with his squad mates, to bark out questions, check identification, and flash lights around for booze.

The other male officer, disconcertingly handsome, his broad-brimmed service cap speckled with rain, demanded I show my ID and empty my pockets. Once it was clear I wasn't concealing anything, he moved aside to pounce on another victim.

When the police finally exited, the music switched back on and the lights dimmed. There was a collective sigh, and everyone went back to dancing. The whole performance lasted maybe fifteen minutes.

Everyone was accustomed to the harassment, but as Marc pushed away from Suzy, panic played across his suddenly pale face. I rushed to console him: Those sham interventions rarely resulted in arrests. But he stalked off and elbowed his way across the dance floor, trailing me in his wake. At the threadbare booth, Marc grabbed his coat and shouted at the Laurel and Hardy duo, insisting it was time to leave.

When Marc and I danced, the buffoons' exaggerated facial expressions had telegraphed their disapproval. Even today, that kind of pissy attitude sets me off. And I found myself blurting that I would give Marc a lift home. The scarecrow acquiesced to the offer, but his pudgy counterpart shot daggers and informed me that he would be doing the honours.

—

Late one August afternoon, seven months after that run-in with the police at the club, I was walking up from Sunset Beach to a party that I had crossed off my calendar twice—only to scribble it back in. For all my new-found sophistication, I considered these affairs a chore: the mindless talk, flitting from person to person, my face aching from smiling. But I was going stir-crazy in my new apartment, friendless while Ray and Randall were off on an open-ended global tour, one financed by auctioning off their art collection.

It was sweltering, and the young men I was pursuing up the hill were dressed only in bathing suits and tank tops. Ahead, at one of the high-rises springing up all along English Bay, our destination was flagged by the array along a balcony rail of still more scantily clad young men.

A group of us crammed into the building's elevator, and, chattering, we ascended. On the twelfth floor, I made my way behind the partygoers down a long hallway. Many of the doors on either side were ajar, men filtering back and forth between them and the apartment at the corridor's end.

At its front door, I glimpsed more men in shorts and bathing suits loitering about in the living room, drinks and cigarettes in hand. Most were slim and tanned, and many seemed acquainted with one another; all were animated. A handsome boy with sun-bleached hair glanced in my direction, his taut body poured into a slinky red Speedo.

"Hi gorgeous! Glad you could make it, Ted."

Terry, the host, rushed over and dragged me into a bear hug. My hands lightly patted his back, then dangled by my sides as

I waited to be released. Terry was tall and heavyset, with a big voice to match. I'd been made amply aware of my physical charms the previous few years, but as far as the "gorgeous" went, I didn't take it personally. Terry called everyone that.

"C'mon in and have a drink—what'll it be?"

"Beer's fine."

I didn't know Terry well, but I'd been running into him frequently, mostly at the Castle, a straight pub on Granville Street that winked at its increasingly homosexual clientele. There he invited me to this "beach bash." From what I had heard, when he wasn't throwing parties or holding court in a bar, Terry travelled between Vancouver and Ottawa on some important government job.

He urged me away from the door so guests could come and go. "Since you didn't bring any beach stuff, you'll find towels in the bathroom. And in the bedroom," Terry said, ogling me up and down, "there's a bathing suit I'm sure you'll have no trouble filling." He slapped me on the rear and sailed off to the fridge.

The men's excited laughter and patter crescendoed, masking Judy Garland's "Stormy Weather" from her Carnegie Hall album. After the song's mournful final measures, someone changed the LP to Ornette Coleman—the jazz high on a hoarse, beboppy sax.

I threaded through the crowd to the balcony overlooking English Bay, feeling out of place, fully clothed among the willowy young men sunning themselves there like cats. I slipped on my shades against the blistering afternoon light, broken in shards shimmering off the water.

Below, Beach Avenue clogged with traffic, bodies sprawled on blankets and towels peppering the adjacent strand. Beyond that, the Vancouver skyline punctuated with building cranes, the Coast Mountains dotted with patches of snow.

"Great view, isn't it?" Terry said as he waylaid me with a bottle of ice-cold beer. Beads of condensation dampened my fingers.

"Sure is." I smiled, but half-heartedly, not wanting my friendliness to be misinterpreted. "Bet the sunsets are fabulous."

"They are." Terry pressed his body against mine. "Stick around. In an hour or so, we can watch it together." I ignored this flirtation, said nothing, and Terry drew back. "In the meantime, you might try mingling. That's what parties are for." He winked, waved to a newcomer, and expertly navigated his bulk through the festivities.

I peered back into the apartment through my sunglasses. After my eyes adjusted, I noted the tasteful Danish modern furniture, the smattering of antique pieces. To my relief, there wasn't a cheap poster of a pricked, nearly nude Saint Sebastian or a facsimile of Michelangelo's hunky *David*. The only whiff of piss-elegance was the two nude male wrestlers bronzed in a frozen embrace on the coffee table in front of the chesterfield.

Slouched on the sofa, his long legs spilling over the seat cushion, was one of the few, along with myself, who wasn't practically undressed. Despite the heat, he wore a brown corduroy jacket and matching slacks. A cigarette limping from one hand, he cradled his drink in the other. His beaklike nose, high forehead, and pale face—handsome in an egghead sort of way—were dominated by black horn-rimmed glasses.

What stands out in memory about him now is his thick, unkempt hair—already completely grey. He gave the impression of being simultaneously young and old. He could have been fifteen years older or even a few years younger than I was—nearly twenty-three.

After a couple of glances, I introduced myself. He peered up at me, the eyes enlarged through the thick lenses suggesting equal parts authority and vulnerability.

"Hello to you," he said, startling me with the unexpected depth of his voice. "Dean." He set his drink beside a golf ball–sized crystal globe on the marble tabletop and offered his hand, palm down as though I were meant to kiss it.

I shook it in the firm manner I had been taught in high school. "I guess we're the only ones here who don't know everybody," I said, watchful again for signs that my friendliness wouldn't be misread as flirtation. Releasing his hand, I noted its slight tremor.

Sipping what appeared to be a gin and tonic, Dean surveyed the room. "You want to know everyone here?"

"Well, no. Not really." I grinned, keeping an eye on the blond boy in the red Speedo as he joined a group of men coming through the front door. "But knowing a few would be nice."

"Well," Dean said, following my gaze, "it appears you're about to commence." He took another nip from his drink, leaned back. "Has it always been Ted? What about Teddy? Or Teddy Boy?"

I gaped at him, disheartened my old name might have shadowed me here. Before I could get a word in, Dean continued. "No, you're hardly a Teddy boy. How about Theodore? Now there's a moniker."

"Ted will do just fine," I replied.

"Good solid Ted." As he spoke, Dean's fist lightly banged out the three words on the marble tabletop. Rattling sharply upon it, the multi-faceted orb of cut glass. "Not to be confused with *stolid*." He smiled as if he were in on some private joke.

I carried on gawking at him, saying nothing.

"Don't mind me. Really." Dean slapped his face lightly, as if admonishing a naughty child. He elevated his almost empty glass. "Afternoon drinks always get to me." He reached for my arm, tugged me down next to him on the couch. "How about removing your sunglasses?" he said, after considering me a moment.

Dizzy from the beer and that abrupt movement, I glanced away. I wondered if talking to this fellow was a mistake, yet resisted the urge to bolt. Pocketing my glasses, feeling suddenly exposed, I shifted on the couch to face Dean.

He smiled. "Ah, there you are! You have such lovely eyes. I'm sure all kinds of people tell you that. And blue grey. Not that usual with brown hair. But why are you still wearing it crewcut? Are you in the forces?"

A needle scratching on vinyl interrupted my reply, putting brash Ornette Coleman out of his misery and signalling another LP change. Dean sat up, cocked his ear. "Thank god that cacophony is over." As he listened intently to the opening bars of the new record, his face broke into a smile. "Ah, Peggy! Now there's a singer."

He scrutinized me through his thick lenses. When I remained silent, he asked, "You don't like Peggy Lee?"

I pulled on my suds and shrugged. "It's not that I don't like her. It's just, there's a weariness to her voice. I can't say what it is, exactly."

Dean reached for a pack of Matinée, shook out the smokes, and offered me one. "A bit of the old ennui, perhaps?"

"Yeah, I guess." I fished in my jeans pocket for my lighter, held the flame up to Dean's cigarette before firing up my own. "Even when she sings fast, there's a kind of fatigue to her voice. I sometimes wonder if she's had enough sleep. Too much of her gets me down."

"Gets you down?" Dean sounded incredulous. "Peggy Lee gets you down? She doesn't get to your heartstrings?"

"No, not really." I gulped my beer, wondering when I formed opinions on singers I hardly listened to and knew next to nothing about. "And I'm not sure I want my heartstrings gotten to."

His eyebrows arched, Dean looked down his nose and said, "Erecting walls around your emotions at such a tender age?"

"I wouldn't put it that way. It's just ... Melancholy singers like Peggy Lee, that's the only music that interests them."

I gestured to the willowy young men still arrayed along the balcony rail. Guys like Michael, Suzy's friend and my art school colleague. And the men Ray and Randall had regularly attempted to foist upon me.

I often ran into their sort at clubs and house parties. Always perfectly coiffed, deeply tanned—which was an achievement in rainy Vancouver. Just then, their bragging references—to art openings and the opera, to jet setting between Frisco, LA, and P-town—were shot through with the word *Mary*, along with knowing winks and showy guffaws. What irked me more than their desperate need for perfection was the feigned indifference overlaying it all, the studied appearance of lassitude. It spoiled what otherwise might be taken for silly, youthful exuberances.

"To me," I said, turning from the young men back to Dean, "all that melancholy, it's just a pose. A thing to avoid facing the real world."

"Whatever that may be." Dean's face was expressionless. "Let me just say that no matter what peculiarities their fans exhibit, those ladies are great vocalists. And they'll be remembered long after whatever was playing a moment ago has been forgotten. In my opinion, their songs bring solace to those who have experienced too much too soon, or perhaps not enough, ever."

A red blur passed inches from my nose. My eyes tracked Speedo boy's moulded globes sauntering out to the balcony. I turned my attention back to Dean and caught his eyes darting from the boy to me.

"Young men," Dean said, holding my gaze. "You were talking about melancholy young men." He took a drag from his cigarette. Though it was only half finished, he butted it in a nearby ashtray, bending it till it broke.

Returning his attention to me, Dean continued. "I take it you're a rock 'n' roll man. Elvis, and all that."

"Well, yeah, sure," I said, aware of needing, for some reason, to regain points. "But there's other stuff happening, more recent, like Bob Dylan."

"Ack!" Dean pressed his palms to both ears, fingers splayed theatrically. "The one who plays harmonica and guitar poorly," he said, lowering his hands to his lap. "He sings through his nose—I can't get past that whine. And I'm never clear about the lyrics."

I didn't always understand Dylan's words, I said. But the ones I did, I loved for their poetry, their honesty. I let Dean know I also loved Gordon Lightfoot, the Kinks, the Animals. Peter, Paul and Mary. Everybody new bursting onto the scene.

A torrent of laughter at the front door—a raft of new arrivals hugging their host. Behind them, a striking dark-haired kid, not in beachwear like the others, separated himself from the group. By a tropical plant whose waxy leaves wound hungrily up a post toward the ceiling, he paused to survey the room, then made a beeline through the chatterboxes to the balcony. The fluidity of his movements drew my eye. I craned my neck to get a better look, but the crowd milling about blocked my view.

Returning to Dean, I found him downing the last of his drink, then unfolding himself from the couch. As he straightened, I was surprised to discover he was well over six feet tall.

Rubbing his stomach, Dean grimaced. "Got to make the bladder gladder." He fixed me with a stare. "Now, don't go away." He snatched my empty beer bottle. "I'll get you another." He lurched off, softly singing something about love in the afternoon, like lilac wine, being heady.

The sound of laughter drew my attention to the balcony, and I again took note of the dark-haired young man. I cast about trying to place him until Dean returned with the drinks. Settling back on the couch with a sigh, he motioned toward the hallway to the washroom. "He's back there."

"Who?" I asked.

"That blond you've been cruising. Quite charming, in an ersatz Tab Hunter kind of way. Definitely not a melancholy young man. He thinks you're cute."

Noting my reddening face, Dean quickly added, "Calm yourself. It was all voluntary on his part. I did not betray your heartstrings." He presented his right hand in a three-fingered salute, as if taking the Boy Scout oath.

"No, no, that's not it," I said. "A guy came in while you were getting drinks. I remembered just now who he is."

"Someone you know?"

"Someone I *knew*. Or thought I was getting to know. Met him last winter at the Montreal Club."

Dean's face tightened—brows knitting, corners of his mouth turning down. "I'm not courageous enough to frequent that part of town. Not to mention I'd find it demeaning."

I picked up the faceted glass globe from the coffee table and stared through it, the room refracting into Technicolor edges. Dean's reaction to the club made me think better of getting into that part of my past. The police raids, the seemingly endless one-night stands, my hookups in public places. He was, after all, still a stranger. An apparently overly squeamish one, at that.

I stubbed out my cigarette and, for courage, drained my beer. Rising to my feet, I excused myself for a moment and barged through the tanned and manicured set on my way to the balcony.

"Marc?"

The mystery man pivoted toward me, a baffled look on his face.

"We've met before," I said.

One brow above his deep-set eyes arched slightly.

"The Montreal Club. Last January."

"Oh, that time." His cheeks reddening, he attempted to cover his embarrassment with a laugh. "I can't believe how naive

I was." Returning his attention to the bay, the smile crumpled, his expression tightening into something like disdain.

"So you got home okay?"

"Oh sure. Sorry my friends gave you a hard time."

"Where you been? I haven't seen you around."

He told me he just returned from working again at the sawmill in the Interior. That in a few days he was starting back at UBC. Moments earlier at Sunset Beach, he trailed a group of guys he presumed were gay up the hill to Terry's apartment.

"A bold move."

He shrugged. "I have to do something. I still hardly know anyone. But I'm not digging the scene."

The sun was gaining now on the horizon. Inside, the din had lowered, the blond boy decamped, along with the tribe of willowy young men. Marc told me he better split. If he missed dinner that evening, the grilling he would get from his folks wouldn't make staying any longer at this party worth the hassle.

I proposed for a second time to give him a lift home, and I was excited when he jumped at the offer. Marc headed to the front door, parting the remaining guests, who, judging by their expressions—some shy, some wolfish—were dazzled by him as much as I was.

Though I thought I had made my intentions clear toward Dean, when I returned to the sofa, a hint of annoyance flickered across his face.

"It appears you've met the love of your night," he said.

"We could go for coffee sometime. Or a drink."

Dean remained silent, his gaze fixed on the figurine of the wrestling men on the coffee table. After searching the room for a pen, I scribbled my phone number on a napkin, tucked its corner under the bronze's base, then pecked him on the cheek.

In the kitchen, I corralled Terry and thanked him for the afternoon. "You'll miss the sunset," he chided as he escorted me out. After administering another bear hug, he released me and gestured toward Dean. "You two seemed pretty absorbed over there. It's been ages since I've seen him so animated."

In the hallway, Marc lounged against the wall, waiting, a half smile on his lips. Before we headed down the corridor, I glanced over my shoulder through the open doorway to see Dean gazing wistfully out at the bay.

I had parked some distance down Beach Avenue, and on our way to my car I reacquainted myself with Marc. He had the solid build I found so captivating at the club the previous winter. And those large, intense hazel eyes. I hadn't noticed, but his resemblance to Wade was striking.

I'd long since banished any thought of Wade, and so as not to diminish my attraction to Marc, I spoiled the comparison. The young man was far shorter and more darkly complected than Wade. Though both sported black hair, Marc's was loosely shaped in waves. In contrast to my former friend's classically sculpted face, Marc's forehead dipped prominently to the bridge of his nose. And his lips weren't tight, uninspiring arcs but full ones, drawing me to kiss them.

Bursting with energy Marc sped ahead while I attempted to keep up. A block before we got to my Beetle, Marc grabbed my hand. Instinctively, I tugged it away. He seemed so disappointed, after making certain no one was around, I snuck my fingers back into his.

Once in the VW, he cupped my face with one hand and leaned over the stick shift to kiss me. For all the sex in the rough I'd had, I was still taken aback by such a public display but succumbed to his hands slipping under my shirt, fondling my chest. As the sun streamed through the VW's windows, he gave the streetscape over my shoulder a look of defiance, then angled in for another kiss.

Out of the corner of my eye, I noticed people approaching and shoved Marc away. I warned him not to get into that in the car. Frowning, he retreated to the opposite side and slumped into his seat.

"If you say so," he said and rolled his eyes.

I let this little dig slide while Marc laid out the location of his parents' house near UBC. The sun dropping behind Vancouver Island blasted into our eyes as I headed west—through the city centre, over Burrard Bridge toward Point Grey.

That suppertime of the evening, the traffic was light, and when not shifting gears, my hand rested lightly on Marc's thigh. As we neared Spanish Banks, he told me he didn't need to be home just yet, suggesting I park in a wooded lot near the one where I first met Randall.

The fog billowing through Burrard Inlet chilled us, so we rolled our windows up—each leaving a small gap at the top. Through it drifted the sound of waves lapping the shoreline and the fishy smell of decomposing kelp. In the tunnel of trees before us, lights on the opposite waterfront trailed through the dusk up the North Shore Mountains to wink out into the advancing mists.

We held hands for a bit, shy suddenly, not speaking. I switched on the radio: the tinny guitar chords and nasal whine of Bob Dylan. That song was everywhere in those days—on record players in friends' apartments, in jukebox diners, there on the radio—"The Times They Are a-Changin'." An anthem of hope. Freedom at last. A new way of being together. And a plea for those who didn't understand to get out of the way.

The beautiful sentiments in that song made me sad, though. They didn't apply to me and Marc, or people like us. We had carved out a pleasant little hidey-hole for ourselves in Vancouver and a few other hot spots, but we were not really meant to be part of the song.

Still, it stirred something in us, and we began to talk. Marc about his studies in biology and his hopes for being accepted to the graduate forestry program. Me about growing up in the Valley and attending art school. He told me art must be interesting—instead of weird, the way most people thought—and wished he too could have grown up outside the city. I let him know the only good thing about being from nowheresville: at university there was no question of living with your parents. For the most part, he said he didn't mind.

It wasn't long before we were necking again. In that confined space, it became almost like a wrestling match. First he gained the advantage, then I did. And then my fly was open—Marc's tongue, the moist warmth—and I was seeing stars. Only it wasn't stars. I opened my eyes and spied in the rear-view mirror flashing lights and realized it was the police.

The windows were steamed over, so they couldn't get a look inside. Only one fat cop, in fact, who took his time shambling toward the car while we straightened ourselves up. When he rapped his knuckles on the glass, I cranked down the window and was blinded by the glare of his flashlight. It skittered off my face across the back seat to linger on Marc.

After this quick inspection, the policeman growled, demanding to know what we were doing, where we lived, where we'd come from. I handed over our licences and my insurance and cooked up a story about studying at my place to get a jump on the fall term—that we'd stopped to talk and listen to music before I drove my friend the rest of the way home. The flashlight's beam raked across our cover: a stack of art books Randall had given me slumped across the back seat.

The cop harangued us then about the perverts who frequented the area, telling us, for our own good, we wouldn't want to be mistaken for something that disgusting. He banged on the car roof for emphasis, turned, and waddled off.

After the patrol car sped away, I saw Marc's face had paled. He was shaking—I guessed because he feared the cop might contact his folks. But when we were on our way again, it was obvious that concern had been overtaken by anger.

All the way to his parents', he raged about the injustice of needing to lie about why we were there and what we were doing. When I told him it was just bad luck—that it was a public place after all—he yelled, "So fucking what!"

Then he threw in my face our harassment at the Montreal Club. That the cops were supposed to protect and serve, not intimidate. Then he railed about how sleazy the bar was, about all our clubs being relegated to the asshole parts of town. As he went on, it was clear he felt I was complicit in the whole thing by not challenging it.

I drove through the misty suburban streets in a stunned silence, shifting gears as if I were on autopilot. Though I was no longer prone to the blues, I felt that familiar darkness tugging at me, for having my connection with Marc interrupted yet again. After a while, all I thought to say was, "Come on, Marc. Please don't let this spoil our evening. We all get popped eventually. That's just the way it is."

He recoiled, crushed back against the passenger door. "It's bullshit! In its own way, this is just as fucked up as what's happening in the States. People there are fighting for their rights. Martin Luther King Jr., and all. When is it going to be our turn?" He shouted this, his face contorted in anger, with hurt.

He insisted I drop him a couple of blocks from his house. Just before he bolted from the car, he bellowed, "Do you think of yourself as some kind of criminal?"

And that was the problem. Beneath the persona I'd crafted of the indifferent man about town, I considered myself—not a criminal, but in some pervasive, barely distinguishable way—as deeply wrong. That feeling clashed with my joy over having liberated myself, even as it fuelled my sexual voraciousness and justified the dingy settings where the acts often took place—as if only in darkness could I know who I was.

I couldn't confess to him that complicated truth—so opposite it seemed from the dogged idealism of his own. Before I could manage some other response, he leapt out, slammed the car door shut—probably startling the whole neighbourhood—then sprinted away.

Even now, I am disappointed in myself for having deadened my shame—through that complacency I so stupidly took for a defence. And I have since confessed to Marc how right he was. And I have marched with him at Pride. Held him close when the world failed so spectacularly to be worthy of him.

But not on that night.

Hoping to redeem myself, or at least to learn how to contact him, I ratcheted the car into gear, barrelled along the street in the direction he ran. There was no one. Only the fog, churning through the tree limbs in the last of the waning light.

going home

"GO ON, THEODORE. You threw it?" Dean took a hit off the joint—his foot tapping out the seconds he held his breath—then through pursed lips exhaled wisps of smoke in my direction. "You threw the camera at your old boyfriend?"

"Wade was never my boyfriend."

"Oh, Theodore. He sure sounds like one to me."

It was the middle of June, and Dean and I were seated at the kitchen table in the top-floor apartment we shared. I was telling the story of the first time I had sex and the fight after, that night at the trailer court in Harrison six years before.

Dean handed me the doobie, and I toked up. We were celebrating my first day at the ad agency, an art school internship I had parlayed after graduation into a full-time job. The marijuana was powerful—Acapulco Gold, Dean's dealer had claimed—so I'd quite blasted off. Through the wavy antique glass of our kitchen window, I gaped at Vancouver's rippled skyline—then, as now, punctuated by building cranes and new towers that seemed to spring up daily.

Dean and I struck up a friendship after our meeting at Terry's "beach" party. We had been roommates for almost a year in my unit in an old, rickety wood-frame house on West Seventh Avenue near Oak. The day Dean moved in, he had few possessions: just some things for the kitchen, and one chair. He brought along a huge stack of books and records, though, and a brand new hi-fi, which was then playing one of his Ladies: Ella Fitzgerald.

"No, I didn't throw the camera at Wade." I let out a laugh, then loosened the tie I was so unaccustomed to wearing, unbuttoned the collar of the stiff new dress shirt Mom had bought me. "But I did take his picture. Lots of them. Turned out there was a whole roll of film in the camera the guy I tricked with gave me. And a flash! He'd slipped quite a few bulbs in my pocket."

Dean began to wheeze. He reached across the kitchen table for the inhaler he always kept at hand. Among his other ailments, Dean had a bad case of asthma. I had given up, though, asking why he persisted in smoking pot.

"You okay?" I said.

He pumped spray down his throat and gulped for air. "Yes, go on."

I took another hit and recounted how dark it had been at the trailer park, Wade just a shadow in the lamplight. I could see well enough, and each time he lunged at me, I snapped another picture. He'd be dazed by the flash, staggering into trash cans and picnic tables while I popped in another bulb.

Wade was there attempting to apologize to his former girlfriend, Maureen, who lived with her parents in a tiny house on the grounds. Her dad rushed over to bluster that if the racket we were making didn't stop, he'd call the cops. Told Wade he meant what he said. He'd do the same if he ever caught Wade skulking around his property again.

After Maureen's father stormed off, Wade and I glared at one another, neither of us sure what to do. I knew he was upset about Maureen dumping him, rather spectacularly, a couple of weeks earlier—over word he meant to remain with his mother's Québécois family in the fall. But what really flustered him, I think, was seeing me so angry. I had rarely ever raised my voice at him.

He cursed me in French, and any time he made a threatening move I shoved the camera in his face. Finally, he withdrew a couple of steps and paused. In the silence, I began to lose my nerve. I had almost worked my way through the supply of bulbs, and I wondered—what if he grabs ahold of me? He'd roughed me up a little at our senior prom. And bulked up as he was from a year of felling trees, if he really wanted, Wade could have done a staggering amount of damage.

Instead of tearing me to pieces, he let out this weird laugh—which scared me even more. He tilted his head back slightly, his features in the lamplight shadowed in deep relief—almost as if they were a figure–ground exercise. And etched there was that scowl of contempt.

"Did he hit you?" Dean said, greedily eyeing the smouldering joint.

"No. He wheeled around and disappeared into the dark. But the way he glared at me hurt more than if he had. I don't think I've ever felt so bad about myself."

"And that's the last you heard from him?"

I brushed my long hair from my cheek and looked through the kitchen window. Each floor of our apartment house had a view, but ours was the most spectacular. I took in Burrard Inlet and False Creek. The North Shore Mountains. In the distance, through the haze, I strained to make out the ghostly silhouette of Vancouver Island.

Dean cleared his throat, stretched out his hand, and poked me after I let the silence accumulate—a habit I had picked up from Wade.

"No, never heard a word," I said, finally begrudging him the joint. "Until the middle of March, when I started getting these letters."

"Beware the Ides of March," Dean growled, his face shrouded in smoke, his voice theatrically deep, ominous. "You know, the whole Sturm und Drang back then with your little friend."

Sadness niggled at me again at that catty reference to Marc and our tempestuous relationship—kindled when we crossed paths a third time the previous fall. I tossed Dean a peevish look as I stroked the envelope in my shirt pocket.

"Yesterday, I received the clincher. After six years, Wade's asking to meet up next month when he gets in from Montreal."

"Well, you know the old saw, Theodore. 'When one door closes, another opens.'"

Perhaps his attempt to lighten the mood by needling me about Marc was Dean's peculiar idea of being helpful. Or maybe it was just pettiness, a cover for jealousy—him never having boyfriends of his own. Whatever it might have been, I refused to take the bait.

Dean inhaled another toke, then exploded in a fit of coughing and wheezing. "What else was in Wade's missive?" he said after the convulsions subsided.

I relayed the excitement that was evident in Wade's last letter—his planned stay at the family farm to visit his mother and new baby brother. And afterward buying a clunker to bum around, like he always wanted, in the American Southwest.

"The guy must have ants in his pants," Dean said. "He's become one of those layabout beatniks, no doubt."

"I guess. He tells me he really digs *On the Road*. Says he's read it twice since he went back east. And Dean, they're called hippies now."

"I stand corrected." Touching the flat of his hand to his forehead, Dean tipped me a quick salute. "Do you still have those photographs you shot of Wade?"

Dean and I danced fingertip with fingertip in exchanging the short, nearly spent joint. Once I'd retrieved it, I toked up. "Burned them all, along with everything else he'd given me. Made a ritual out of it end of the summer, after he lit out for Quebec."

"Such a drama queen." Dean spun the inhaler on the tabletop as he lost himself in the scene framed in the window. "Well, Theodore?" he said at last. "Are you going to see him?"

I shrugged. "I don't know. I mean, why ..."

"... stir it all up again?" Dean loved jumping in and completing other people's sentences.

"Something like that." I passed the joint back to him.

After taking a cautious puff, Dean hung the lit end of the cigarette over the edge of the table, then rummaged through the stack of newspapers on its Formica top. "FLQ bombings in Montreal, the fallout over those murders in Mississippi. And what are the Americans doing in Vietnam, anyway?"

"Pretty depressing stuff."

"Well, there's this." From the bottom of the pile, he eased out last year's infamous issue of *Maclean's*, folded open at the article that had caused such a fuss. "The Homosexual Next Door."

"Who knew," I said, "we're just like everyone else."

"Don't be cynical, Theodore. People think this might be the start of something."

As it turned out, it was. You can draw a straight line from that magazine piece to me here in bed now—my husband, the American, napping beside me. Back then, though, I could be forgiven for my cynicism about the article's impact. Police harassment of our bars and clubs had been especially heavy handed the year the article was published. And not long before that, the last British Columbian ever to be executed was a man whose sentence likely would have been commuted had he not been homosexual.

Dean ran his finger down the tight column of sentences, pretending to reread the *Maclean's* article. And perhaps he did, the paragraphs filling him with hope. But from the way he snuck sidelong glances at me, I suspected he was dying to hear more about Wade.

He finally abandoned the ruse, tossing the magazine back on the stack. "So what did you see in your friend, anyway? From what you've told me so far, he appears to be a jerk."

I shook off my pessimism to answer. "He was a total jock. Incredibly handsome."

"Sounds like a dream, Theodore, but there had to be more to it than that."

Words could be such a struggle back then. No wonder I'd elected to go to art school. And Dean gawking at me expectantly—giving me his wise old owl look through the thick lenses of his glasses—was only making it worse. I opened my mouth, afraid nothing would come out. But the words did start. At first haltingly, then something in me broke loose.

I explained that despite Wade's popularity in high school, he was at his core just as much a loner as I. We found safety in each other's company, hitching all over the Valley. Going hiking and camping. Trucking up logging roads with other kids and getting shit-faced drunk.

After the Agassiz bridge was completed, we even made it to Vancouver. I browsed the record stores and bookshops while he flirted with girls. I hadn't been the only one who found him attractive. And sure, I said, he had a temper that sometimes made him act aggressively, but he was funny too, often incredibly gentle.

I retrieved the short joint from the table, relit it, and took a final draught. "What drew me to him was his intensity and gutsiness. He didn't appear to give two shits about anything—not me, his mom, his girlfriend, or, most of all, school. Yet you knew he did. That gave him a kind of ..."

"... magic?" Dean said.

"Magic, yeah. The magic Wade has," I said. "Had."

"Sensitive straight boys, they'll get you every time."

I chuckled, wet my fingers on my tongue, and pinched out the smouldering roach. "Sensitive straight boys shouldn't be allowed."

"Still," Dean said, "the question stands."

"I don't know. What would be the point of seeing him again? What if none of that magic exists anymore? We're both probably very different now."

Dean scrutinized me a few moments before breaking the silence. "Do we ever really change, Theodore? Sure, maybe Wade's got this beer belly now. Maybe his swagger's deflated a notch. You know, the regrets of an aging high school sports stud. But what about the man behind the curtain? Isn't what's hidden from view the thing that draws you to art?"

Wade's sudden urge to reconnect did intrigue me. He wrote that he had changed, and I wondered where we each stood on the path to maturity. Boyhood emotions lingered, but I was unsure what I felt for him. One thing was certain: Since receiving those letters, he had returned front and centre in my mind.

Dean fidgeted with his inhaler, stared out the window. Framed in the wavy glass, sailboats skimmed among the hulking cargo ships anchored in English Bay. Dean stirred after another moment of stoned silence.

"Make up your mind, Theodore," he said. "Are you going to see him or no?"

—

I was driving my VW eastbound along the roller-coaster stretch of Highway 1, feeling an orchestra should be playing "Ode to Joy." With the same delight the music gives me, I bounded hill after hill, spying the Fraser's wide flood plain—the berry and poultry farms, the rows of electric-green corn. All checkerboarded by cedar and fir windbreaks, echoes of the old-growth forest long gone.

I was somewhere near Langley, I figure. Since the road skirts the river towns, until I hit the Abbotsford cut-off, I'm never sure exactly where I am. It was one Saturday the middle of July, that's certain, and I was driving my old Beetle to Harrison Hot Springs. Before their deaths, every few weeks I made that trek to visit my parents, who were alone in our small house after I fled to Vancouver. Earlier, I'd written Wade I'd be in Harrison that weekend and planned to pay him a visit.

I geared down to ascend the last of the lazy hills. Cars whizzed by, and when I glanced over at them, it appeared as if I were travelling backward. I am struck now by the other reason I made those pilgrimages. Though I am unable to articulate it precisely, it has to do with landscape and memory.

It seems strange Dean wasn't accompanying me on that trip—one he had made many times over the preceding year—but he was still too ill to travel.

When he didn't come out of his room the previous day, I found him bent over, collapsed on the edge of his bed, cradling his head in his hands, rocking slowly and moaning. He was hiding in there with one of his migraines, wearing sunglasses, all the blinds down and the lights off.

His helplessness brought out my protective instincts, which he ignored. He declined all the food I pressed upon him—since he was vomiting everything anyway. Waved off my pleas for him to go to the emergency room or at least to call a doctor. He said he'd been through all that—just swallowed painkillers that barely helped and some useless pills from the health food store.

He swore he was fine, though it was clear he was not. By the time the episode ended, we were both so shaken we started to cry. "It's okay, baby," he whispered, after he had collected himself. "I think we've won this round."

It astonishes me how Dean loved these visits to my little hometown. Just as Joanne and my mother once did, Dean spent most of his time conversing with Mom about books, as well as passing on newspapers and magazines with "Read This!" and "Highly Recommended!" scrawled all over the margins.

At times I experienced twinges of envy at how easily they communicated. Dean was able to evoke ideas and thoughts that must have incubated for years in Mom. Since her only companion in that quiet, isolated household was a low-key Irishman whose love of words extended no further than telling off-colour tales at the pub.

Dean had practically adopted our family, his parents having all but abandoned him when they discovered he was gay. Perhaps that loss contributed to his excitement when I mentioned I needed a roommate to cut expenses during my final year of art school. I confessed to him that the neighbourhood and apartment house had both seen better days and that the communal bathroom was on the ground floor, requiring a trek down three flights of creaky stairs. But I also let him know that the other tenants were very cool kids. That the place was kept reasonably clean and in good order by its crusty old landlady. It surprised me when Dean agreed to my offer, saying it sounded just like heaven.

Though our apartment was small, we got along. When I was still in art school, during the day I studied in my room, in class, or in Ray's studio while Dean worked at a bookstore. After I graduated the end of May—except for the week I was laid up by the business with Marc—I toiled at the agency on workdays. And on nights when I wasn't out on the prowl, I mostly had the rooms to myself as Dean often disappeared mysteriously.

At first, I supposed he was at a pub or a steam bath. But when I asked, he said he never went to either. Since he didn't bring anyone home, I guessed he was having sex in parks or cars, but he denied that too. I was beginning to wonder if he even had an interest in guys when one evening at the Vancouver Art Gallery I found him shadowing an extraordinarily handsome man from room to room. Dean made no attempt to attract the fellow's attention—in fact, it became obvious Dean didn't want to be seen.

I kept a close eye on them both until Dean, at a distance, tailed the man out the museum's front door. At this point, his quarry grabbed a cab, and minutes later Dean was hailing one of his own, frantically pointing his driver in the direction of the car the man had just taken.

As I usually did, I had on hand my trusty camera, the present I'd been given that summer night I first got laid. So, I snapped a few quick shots of Dean scrambling into the cab. After hurrying home, I developed the film in the broom closet that doubled as my makeshift darkroom. The prints came out all askew, with Dean crowded into the margins and corners.

When he returned late that night, bruises marked his face and arms, and although he joked about doorknobs, it was clear he had run into something more sinister.

When I reached the Abbotsford exit, I shifted my VW from fourth to third gear and veered onto the off-ramp, then barrelled north across the valley chequered with farms. The wind scouring across the open window raked my hair against the nape of my neck.

There had been the promise of rain the whole trip, and now that I was closer to the mountains, I drove in and out of showers.

A blanket of clouds uncoiled from above the forested hills ahead, but piercing it every so often sunbursts threw into relief portions of the valley. Over all of this presided Mount Cheam, in the bowl at its centre a snow angel cradled to its heart.

I had attempted to instill in Dean a love for this landscape, to lure him into the woods to admire my favourite childhood haunts. Because of his illnesses, though, any sort of physical activity was out of the question. Nature, he maintained, was best witnessed in zoos or in back issues of *National Geographic*.

That hadn't been the case with the ever-elusive Marc. In fact, he seemed only to come alive outdoors. During our brief fling after reconnecting the previous fall, on our trips to Harrison Marc and I often stomped up Mount Woodside, where Wade and I had so many good times. And several chilly winter afternoons up Bear Mountain, Marc and I smoked up, warmed our stiff fingers with our breath, and hastily jerked each other off. An enactment of what I had always fantasized doing there with Wade.

After Marc's disappearance the night of Terry's "beach" party, I searched for him—at the Montreal Club, the Castle, that stretch of shoreline tunnelled in the trees near Spanish Banks where the cop had hassled us.

I even wore out my welcome with Joanne in my quest to find Marc at UBC—shadowing her daily to classes, buying beers I couldn't afford at the student union for her and her gang of grad school literati.

There were times I saw a dark-haired, compact fellow with a lively gait soldiering up Main Mall. I'd rush ahead and tap him on the shoulder, only to find, when he wheeled around, a scowl on the face of a stranger.

In the end, I hadn't needed to cast so wide a net.

The house on West Seventh where Dean and I lived was famous for its parties. They were tremendous smoke-a-thons, since most of us kids were seriously getting into pot. The Halloween bash after Marc's vanishing act had been a real blowout. Everyone had come as their favourite medical condition.

I was jaundice. My hair concealed under a yellow swim cap, I wore only a yellow Speedo, my body slathered similarly head to toe with something Suzy from art school concocted.

By then, she had moved into the large ground-floor apartment and was shacked up with that tough gal I'd seen her with in January. The two were rooming with Michael, my good-looking art school classmate, who they had been dancing with at the club. He crashed in a room off the kitchen, a closet really, barely big enough to accommodate a single mattress, along with his colourful clothes arrayed along a pole hung from the ceiling.

At the Halloween party, Suzy was costumed in black leotards with charcoal gauze wings stretched over a coat hanger frame—a tsetse fly, she told us, mother of the sleeping sickness. Michael was shrouded in a beige plastic suit holder, his head concealed behind a bulbous papier mâché glans that oozed a gonorrheal pus. Dean made a late appearance, a baby doll sewn onto an old shirt, his vestigial twin.

Joanne, as a slutty nurse, sported a surgical mask bungeed under her chin and an old-school angled cap. Batwing-blackened eyes, scarlet lipstick, and a feather boa of a matching colour that framed her nursing uniform's plunging neckline.

Plodding alongside her was her brick of a man, pre-med, looking ill at ease despite his air of square-jawed masculinity. In a failure of imagination, he wore a crisply pressed white lab coat, a stethoscope pilfered from school dangling from his neck.

He was a total square, Joanne had confessed to me a few weeks before over a late-night phone call. Though she had trashed her bras in solidarity with women's lib, having experienced so much instability—squabbling parents, a hotelier's peripatetic life—she now craved authority. Which this boneheaded new boyfriend provided in spades.

As for me, that night was one of the wildest times I'd ever had—completely plastered on Rusty Nails on top of the pot. I was dancing my ass off to the Beatles' "Twist and Shout"—all of us kids singing a high-pitched "woooo" each time the boys hit their vocal trademark—when I spied the sturdy body burned into my memory silhouetted in an open doorway.

Marc, his coat dangling jauntily from one hand onto the floorboards.

I rushed with open arms to embrace him, fairly falling-down drunk and practically naked, smeared all over in yellow. Marc recoiled in confusion. It wasn't long, though, before I ran off the kids smoking in the downstairs bathroom, and Marc and I were showering together, Suzy's concoction sluicing down our naked bodies, circling the drain.

After that, Marc became a fixture at our apartment house. A veritable moving feast, dropping by, day or night—bopping in and out of everybody's apartments to chat, bounding up the stairs to hang with Dean and me.

He was no longer a firebrand. Without a quick pathway to gay rights, Marc was of the mind that the only course left him was to practise a profound hedonism. Which meant sometimes sleeping upstairs with me, sometimes downstairs with Michael—who was as enamoured with him as I was. Even when he and Michael screwed, often as not Marc slinked into my bed as I dozed off and nuzzled up to go another round or two.

Why did he—and people like Wade and Paul—have so much energy when I possessed so little? If it wasn't for school, work, and my hormone-overloaded body, I'd happily spend days in our apartment painting or reading on the couch. And, Dean excepted, why did I always align myself with high-energy people—and why were they so attracted to me?

Mother even joked about Marc being a "jackrabbit" on one of the occasions I brought him to our little house in Harrison. She could be so observant and so clueless—Marc and I humping away upstairs in my bedroom, she and Dad conked out directly below.

Being with Marc was everything I'd dreamed of—that fantasy life I'd constructed with Paul, paired with the sensation of homecoming I often experienced with Wade. Only with lots of sex.

I was so enamoured with Marc that I couldn't resist proclaiming the affair to my parents, which meant finally coming out to them. Over martinis, before Christmas dinner, no less. For the first time they included me in their traditional cocktail toast, one my sober-minded parents did only at special occasions. With the gin stirring up feelings for this rite of passage, for Marc, I blurted it all out.

Mom accepted the news with her stoic remove, which an unprecedented second martini enhanced. She said she figured something was up since, other than Joanne, I never paid much attention to girls. Dad was quiet all through supper. Over dessert he offered that he had an uncle in Ireland "that way"—a good-enough sort—and left it at that.

Bringing everything into the open seemed to jinx what there was between myself and Marc. For as the winter edged into spring, the closer I felt to him, the further he withdrew, sacking out with Michael more and more.

That first letter from Wade stirred up my sentimental feelings, and with them came an awareness that the hard-boiled attitude I'd cultivated in my relations with men was a sham. A denial of my desperate longing for union.

So, on that fateful mid-March night, I found myself pleading with Marc not to go downstairs to sleep with Michael. He sat up in bed and scowled, said emotional intensity was a waste of time. He was way too young, with too much ahead of him to indulge in it.

When I told him I couldn't block up my feelings inside anymore—when I confessed I loved him—he leapt up, gathered his clothing, and shut the door behind him. Ever so gently, as I'd harped on him to do, so as not to wake Dean. With each thud of his footsteps descending the stairs, a piece of myself ripped away.

Though I heard from Suzy that he and Michael were still hooking up, Marc stopped visiting Dean and me. My final-year projects were a bear—a large and ambitious cut-paper photo collage, a clay sculpture—which required me to hunker in the studio night and day. This prevented me from moping over Marc, and though it was a lacklustre showing, I managed to pull off the assignments.

One morning the end of May, soon after my graduation from school, Michael pounded on our apartment door. He stood in the opening, a peacock whose wild red and gold patterned dashiki hung atop a pair of crisp white bell-bottoms. He was red faced from crying, screaming that it was my fault—me and my "nature boy" shit, all those hikes in the Valley with Marc. When I barked at him to stop, saying I hadn't a clue what he meant, he told me Marc had just decamped for the remote Quetico Provincial Park—for a whole year of fieldwork.

I realized then how much I loathed Michael, his fastidiousness and clownish fashions. Without defending myself, I slammed the door in his face, undressed, and took to bed. As there were a couple of weeks before my advertising job began, I yielded finally to my dejection over losing Marc yet again.

I would go on to lose him several times more, on each occasion the sting diminishing a little, but then the loss overwhelmed me. I wallowed under the covers, rarely eating, never bathing. My underclothes and bedsheets stank.

On and off each day, I phoned Joanne in hopes for a little tough talk and commiseration. She'd been living in Toronto since January, having pursued her mother there after her parents' divorce. Along the way, Joanne gave up on her grad degree in English lit and jilted her fiancé—abandoning the bore at City Hall holding their never-to-be-registered marriage licence.

I couldn't reach her on the phone, though. She was always out liberating herself, she'd informed me—smoking up with draft dodgers, digging Yorkville's hippie scene, protesting the Vietnam War. If she had picked up, I wasn't certain what I'd tell her. I hadn't yet confessed the truth about myself. An unnecessary caginess, since in hindsight it's clear most everyone in her college crowd was gay.

To pass the time while confined in bed, I succumbed to the old habit of fantasy, spinning scenarios of being Marc's research assistant, the two of us navigating the lakes at the provincial park. Days we glided our canoe past moss-covered shores dotted with stunted red pine, past cliff faces daubed with silver and black rock tripe bouquets. Nights we spent lovemaking at beachside campsites—always under a full moon—the braided shadows of tree limbs embossed on the sand.

I survived off these dreams for the better part of a week. Until one afternoon Dean marched into my room and yanked back the covers, proclaiming our apartment only required one invalid and he had already filled the position.

Crossing the Mission bridge that spans the Fraser, I ground to a stop at the light. When it flashed green, I jerked the car into gear, sped east along the two-lane Lougheed Highway. Passed through Dewdney in a blink, zipped by Lake Errock and the Sasquatch Inn. Glimpsing the big river shimmer through backlit alder and maple bordering the freshly plowed fields, I felt the anxieties of the city and freeway fade away.

But the road soon squeezed between tall cliffs and the marsh that edges the broad curve of the Harrison River, and this peace was shattered by memories and concerns spawned by the letters from Wade.

For this is the spot where he and I hitched the ride from the man who I let grope me—the fall I was sixteen, and Wade and I played hooky. As if on cue, a young man appeared on the opposite side of the highway, his back to me, thumb out to an oncoming car. He could have been Wade—the short dark hair and height were similar. He wasn't, of course. And when I checked in the side mirror, the car had already passed him by, and he had turned and was trudging on.

In the rear-view mirror, I examined my face, hoping to travel the continuum from the men we had become to the boys we were nine years before. The vision was muddied, though, by how thoroughly I'd driven my experiences with Wade from my mind. Casting about for something more recent also yielded nothing, since on my trips to Harrison I never once stopped at his parents' farm to inquire how he was. I told myself I was no longer the person who cared about Wade.

Then came his first letter.

> Montreal
> March 10, 1965
> Dear Teddy,
>
> Got your address from your mom. She tells me you're at art school in Vancouver, final year I think she said. Who'da thought—with no art taught in our school after Grade 8.

Me, I'm still keeping the faith here with Mom's family. Working at my uncle's insurance company. Entry-level desk job, if you can believe that.

I'll make this short, as I don't know if you want to write me or even know me anymore.

I'm sorry for the shitty things I said to you at the prom. Plus, how I acted that night at the trailer court. I mean, I was loaded for bear after fighting with Maureen's dad. But no cause to take it out on you.

To cut to the chase, in some fucked-up way, I got off on you liking me. I didn't want sex, but I really dug you admiring me. Growing up, I didn't have much of that.

No worries if you don't get back. But I wanted to let you know being out here has opened my eyes. I've grown up a bit.

I hope you do write, Teddy. You were my best friend during those lousy years in high school, and when I think back on it, most of the good times were spent with you.

Still your friend, I hope,
Wade

I refused to read that letter when I saw the name scrawled above the return address. Hid it at the back of a drawer in my study desk, neglected it while I scrambled to salvage the big photo collage. One night in a drunken fit over the debacle with Marc, I had clawed from the canvas fistfuls of paper photos and glue—convinced of the worthlessness of the composition and my life.

Nearly two weeks passed before I came upon Wade's letter. For so long after our falling-out, I'd cast him as a cardboard cut-out villain. I cried, though, when I finally read it and took in the heartfelt emotions, the regrets underlying his casual tone.

And thinking how he carried those through the years, as I banked toward the Harrison River bridge, other memories and regrets came spilling out.

I saw us as kids.

We were all packed in the gym.

Music blared over the speakers, and everyone was dancing and carrying on.

It was May 1959, the night of our high school grad prom, our final group bash before we all headed out into the unknown. The girls wore poofy, brightly coloured chiffon dresses. All us guys were still in the jackets and ties worn for the graduation ceremony earlier that day. For most, it was the first time we had ever been in suits.

The supper club at the resort was shuttered for the weekend—burst pipes, a flooded kitchen—so for the prom the school hired their old fogey band on the cheap. The singer smiled too broadly, her heavily made-up face appearing as if it were a plaster cast. She was droning a Rosemary Clooney song Mom was crazy about, one that made us kids roll our eyes, it was so boring.

Wade had come in from Silver River camp for the prom and was on the other side of the gym dancing with Maureen, who was wearing his old varsity jacket. Always bucking the trend, he sported tight jeans and a biker jacket, just a T-shirt underneath that showed off his chest.

From the way Maureen clung to him, I assumed she'd heard the rumours about Wade relocating to Montreal. Two inches taller than him, she had one hand slung over his shoulder, the other snaking under his armpit to clasp her wrist—as a wrestler might before pinning an opponent.

I was doing the opposite, stiff-arming Joanne at a suitable distance. We were buddies, of course. Still, I kept praying that slow song would end. All the while, my eyes darted to Wade.

I'd been attempting to gauge the best time to talk to him, something for a year we had barely done.

Every so often graduates and their dates slipped out the double doors and around behind the gym for a smoke and beer or whatever else anyone could sneak in. Earlier that week, I'd hit up the bootlegger for a mickey of rye, something that could be easily concealed yet still pack a wallop.

Finally, the song concluded. When Wade headed for the doors, I let Joanne know I'd be right back and pursued him into the parking lot. There, he skulked in a dark corner, leaning against the hood of a car. After downing the last of his beer, he hurled the bottle into the bushes, then thundered a phlegmy, guttural burp.

"Hey, Wade," I said. I couldn't believe how nervous I was.

Rotating his head slightly, he eyeballed me askance but said nothing.

I slipped my peace offering from out of my jacket. "Drink? Let's have a drink. Maybe talk." I attempted to keep my voice from shaking.

His face rigid in the glare of a floodlight, he scrutinized me for what seemed a long time. I felt foolish standing there, holding out the bottle. I sensed an unsettling disconnection as well. For in place of the belonging I so often experienced in his company, with his rigid masculine posturing, his flinty expression, I felt threatened instead. In the presence of a total stranger.

At the gym door, a teacher glowered at us. Then I heard footsteps—some of our classmates making their way across the parking lot. I eased the bottle into my coat pocket and turned to Wade. A weird smile played over his lips.

"Sure," he said, "but let's get away from these assholes."

Wade launched himself off the car, wheeled around, and strode toward the old bus shed behind the far end of the school. It was where kids snuck off to smoke and drink or sometimes neck. He hauled back the sliding door, just enough for us to wedge ourselves through the gap. In the faint stream of light angling through a high window, three yellow buses hunkered side by side.

"Let's have it." Wade presented his hand for the bottle. He downed a swig, grimaced. He thrust it back, and I took a sip.

"So what do you want to talk about?" Wade said.

"I don't know. I mean … I heard the big news. About Montreal. Your mom must be excited." The halting sentences betrayed my fear of confronting what I really wanted to address: the rift between us.

He snatched the bottle from my hand, then slouched against one of the buses. After chugging half the remaining liquor and coughing up half of that, he wiped his mouth on the sleeve of his jacket.

"It's just … well," I said, extending my hand for the bottle, "with us in the bush all summer and me taking off to Vancouver. We might not see each other—for a long time."

He jerked the flask from my grasp, and I shrank back.

"You know what I think," he said, lurching off the bus and advancing toward me. "You wanted to get me alone in here, just like you wanted all those other times."

"Wait, no. You're the one who …"

"You're the one who followed me out to the fucking parking lot. And now you want to do with me like that guy did to you in the Bel Air. Isn't that right?"

I'd never heard Wade speak with this undertone of hatred. With his eyes glazed, his face pinched with that habitual expression of disdain, I could barely look at him.

"Wade, stop it. What's the matter with you? You know that's not true."

"Like fuck it's not. You think I don't see you watching me? All the fucking time, you're watching me. At first, I couldn't figure it out, but now I know. You're a fuckin' …"

"Wade, please." My voice trembled, my desire to reconnect morphing into something hideous. "I just want to talk before we leave, that's all. Like we used to, all the times we gabbed about our plans after graduation."

With his free hand, he gripped the lapel of my jacket, swung me around, then slammed me against the bus. The air forced from my lungs, my head jerked back, smashing against metal. His face scowled inches from mine. "All that time, all that fucking time. Be honest for once. Why were you really with me?"

"Because ... because ..." I felt the words swell, attempting to burst out, but it was as if I were drowning—underwater again in one of those dreams I used to have—desperately shouting but with no sound.

Releasing me, Wade stepped a few paces away and stood motionless—eyes glistening, lips curled. For a moment, I feared he would strike. I wished for that, my confusion was so great. I longed for the blow that would redeem that moment, bridge—even in a twisted way—the gap that persisted between us.

Instead, Wade slowly held out the flask as if to return it, but his fingers spread and he let the bottle drop. Whipping around, he strode out of the shed, shattered glass crunching beneath his boots.

I was jogged from this recollection by the *thunk-thunk* of wheels crossing the Harrison River bridge. I slipped the car into a viewpoint and switched off the engine. In the mirrors, the sight of Mount Woodside sparked yet more memories. Wade and me tramping up its northern and eastern slopes. The crazy quilt of farm plots below, each edged by an irrigation ditch or hedgerow. Us sprawled on a rocky outcrop up top, sun warming our tired limbs, his head resting lightly on my thigh.

I lowered my forehead to the steering wheel. My eyes stung with tears as I shut them. It was a mistake trying to forget Wade. But after that fight and the following one at the trailer court, for so long my mind was locked against him, my emotions numbed. Then I would feel intense anger, then helplessness, before returning to neutral once more—all in an endless loop.

After recovering from reading Wade's first letter, I had my hands full scissoring photos into triangles and squares, pasting that collage back together—dizzy and slightly nauseous from the rubber cement. With all that—and feeling hurt and anger over Michael and Marc's enthusiastic coupling downstairs—I again forced myself to forget about Wade.

It wasn't until mid-April that I begrudged him the shortest of replies—confirming I was gay but being cagey about the details of my life in Vancouver. Letting him know I was going by Ted now. And sure, I wrote, why not let bygones be bygones? I didn't expect it to cost me anything.

End of April, though, I received a second letter.

> Montreal
> April 30, 1965
> Dear Ted,
>
> Good to hear from you, old friend! Sure glad you're not holding on to any hard feelings.
>
> More than I can say for Maureen. I was clear about not wanting to get married. That summer after the prom, though, she got me see-sawing about staying put here after my Paquette family kumbaya. She made some real convincing arguments against it—if you get my drift. Guess I got her hopes up. 'Cause when I finally laid it on her, she fucking went ballistic.
>
> My news pissed my old man right off as well. Bastard figured I'd slink back from Quebec and work

on his stinking farm. I'll give it to him: He never calls it quits on that piece-of-shit parcel of land.

Bad blood all round, I'm afraid.

Twenty years my mom was broke up here with her family. Made me nervous as hell about meeting them. Would have bailed on the deal if she hadn't wanted it so bad.

There was no reason to worry, though. At the Gare Centrale, my aunt Lise was so excited to see me, she nearly jumped out of her skin. She threw a blowout at her place where all the Paquettes—my other aunts, uncles, a zillion cousins—drank themselves silly and oohed and aahed over me.

My grandfather gave me the stink eye, though. Grumbled something in his farmer Québécois I couldn't make heads or tails of. Wouldn't shake my hand either.

I took to my corner a few days to pout. Lise said I've got a problem with authority figures, which got me to sucking up to my grandfather big time, impressing him with all that French Mom crammed into me.

With that, the old man finally chilled. He's pretty decent, actually, not the religious nutjob I thought he was. These days I roll him in his wheelchair out back of the house, sneak him whisky and cigarettes. He's teaching me how to tell dirty jokes in French.

He and Mom are even speaking now. Though it'll probably tee off Dad, she plans to visit Montreal this fall to show off her January surprise, my new baby brother.

So, I've pretty much served my purpose here. Thinking about next moves. My uncle wants to promote me. Says I have natural ability. But I can't see myself in friggin' insurance, can you? Plus, it's probably time to get the hell out of Dodge. Another bomb went off downtown this morning. And they call it the Quiet Revolution!

Sorry for going on, but I always could talk about stuff easy with you.

So, what is it you're getting up to? I promise, I'm not going to be all shocked or self-righteous. You can tell me anything.

Your friend,

Wade

Though touched by his letter, I hadn't the time or inclination to respond to it or his subsequent one. I threw myself into my project for sculpture class, an abstract clay face that needed maquette after maquette to get right. I willed myself to erase from my mind both Marc and Wade, wanting to bleed from my life every unnecessary complication.

In the car, I opened my eyes and sat upright. Through my tears, the Valley was blurred, as if viewed from behind mottled glass. The curve too of the distant Cascades softening into the blue of the sky. And far off to the right, I could make out the line across the mouth of the Harrison River. There, its blue waters churned and eddied against the muddy Fraser before losing themselves in its massive flow. I was buoyed suddenly by its beauty, by this ancient order of transformation.

I tried to picture what shape my life might take should I embrace complexity and reconcile myself with my past. Not only with these two men, or Paul, but with the persistent shadow of a boyhood endured in this valley in such loneliness.

No longer willing to resort to fantasizing, my conjectures were scattered and dim. The old heaviness of spirit revisited me, a leaden sensation in my face, my limbs. But beneath it, I detected a flicker of excitement. Anticipating that in resignation, there would be some movement toward the better, toward ease. Just not yet understanding how it might come.

At this, my shoulders loosened, the muscles in my face relaxed. I blinked the remaining tears away and pulled the car out of the viewpoint. Shifting into third, I descended Mount Woodside's long tunnel of trees.

Through the loose weave of foliage, on the plain below I glimpsed Wade's family's farm. Most of it lay in the northern shadow of a wooded hill that hindered crops from fully maturing, a pitiful operation going nowhere. Surrounding their land were Dutch and German dairy farms—sunlit, tidy, well drained, and productive.

When I reached the valley floor, I slowed the car and began to swerve onto the road that led to his family's property. At the last minute I lost my nerve, wrenching the steering wheel to the left, forcing the car back onto the highway.

It was late afternoon when I pulled down the drive of the cottage in Harrison and stationed the Beetle behind my father's trusty Studebaker. I found him up a ladder in the big holly tree in the backyard—in coveralls, gloved and goggled, rigging yet another TV antenna. Before everyone got cable, reception was particularly bad in our small town, hemmed in as it is between mountains to the east and west. Our only television stations back then were the CBC and one from Bellingham, just across the line.

Dad was an inveterate tinkerer. In his early years, he was a pipefitter at the Belfast shipyards. Plus, working for so long as a handyman at the resort. So, in an attempt to bring in better reception, he was creating an elaborate arrangement of TV aerials—all of which Mom called bloody eyesores. He had located them on the roof, in the front and back yards, and by then even up the old holly tree. For all his work that day, it would still be ghosts and static flitting across the screen.

He scampered down the ladder and shucked off his goggles and gloves, angry red scratches scrawled, even so, on his face and hands. He gave me a quick hug. "Talk to your mother for me, please." I was shocked by the desperation I detected in his voice.

Inside, Mom was furious. I had never seen her so worked up. Apparently, it was over some remark Dad had made about Jews. She never could stand any sort of prejudice. After I calmed her down, my father tossed his protective gear on the kitchen table, then knelt to grovel at her feet, apologizing for being a "feckin' eejit."

Now she was placated, and the evening began to cool, Mom and I settled into chairs on the back deck and surveyed the garden she lovingly maintained. Through the open kitchen windows came the sound of ice cubes rattling in a metal shaker. Then silence, then the screen door slammed. On the low table between Mom and me, Dad deposited a tray on which glistened the flared glasses containing three martinis.

When I asked about the special occasion, Dad swept his hand through the air, marking the mountain's forested ridge ablaze in the setting sun. The hydrangea blossoms, their cauliflower-like centres nestled in rings of purple flowers. The fronds of Solomon's seal, each underside fringed with pale stems where tiny bells once hung. Lastly, he motioned to Mom.

My mother nodded, elevated her glass. "We may be poor," she said, clinking it against Dad's glass and mine. "But we're civilized."

—

Under a clear sky the following morning, the sun streamed over the glassy lake and stripped the chill from the air. The day, the CBC had predicted, would be a scorcher.

Beyond the white pickets at the front of the house, the first of the beachgoers were positioning their station wagons. Young Punjabi men in baseball caps and jeans and their brightly turbaned fathers wrangled ice chests and folding chairs while smartly dressed women in gauzy head scarves corralled children.

For my first day home: Mom's special breakfast of flapjacks, eggs over easy, and bacon—just she and me that morning, Dad having departed earlier for work at the town's resort. She fairly burst with pride—and, I'm certain, considerable relief—over my recent graduation and the new job, my first, at the advertising studio.

After cleaning up from breakfast, on the back porch she kissed my cheek and wished me well. We'd never spoken of my falling-out with Wade, but she intuited the importance of my visit that morning.

As I drove the two-lane road out of town, my fear over reconnecting with my former friend gave way to the flicker of excitement I experienced the day earlier about what might lie in store. Where the highway took a wide curve as it neared Agassiz, I slipped past hayfields, their columns of freshly cut grass greying in the summer sun.

At Wade's ramshackle clapboard house, his mother greeted me, the new baby draped over one shoulder fast asleep. Through the open doorway, I caught sight of the kitchen cluttered with racks of washing and took in the faint scent of sour diapers and piss.

A short woman with a broad pale face, Wade's mother was stouter than I remembered and wore a shapeless housedress patterned with sprays of dull-brown flowers. Though in her early forties, she appeared much older—everything about her seeming worn and plain. A short pageboy cut was her only concession to appearance.

A smile brightened her face when she recognized me, and she made much of how I had changed. "I believe that my son, he is over there, raking the hay," she said, her French Canadian accent as strong as ever, with the *h* silent and *th* pronounced with a *d*. She pointed to the field in the shadow of the hill, adding that Wade was wishing very much that I would come by.

As I approached, he was standing on the seat of a tractor, his dark hair draped over his shoulders, his binoculars trained on a hawk gyring in a current high in the sky. He sported an impossibly bushy moustache—I've teased him about it for years now—like some B movie tough guy. His body was no longer that of the lithe basketball player I first met, but the strapping tree faller. His musculature had softened, though, and was capped by a considerable paunch.

I halted a moment on the cut grass near the edge of the shadow that bisected the plot he had been windrowing. My nervousness over this meeting returned, the not-knowing making me queasy. I collected myself, called out his name, and was met by my old delight in witnessing his movements: his pivot on the seat and leap from the tractor in a single bound.

He strode toward me, grinning broadly, the field glasses dangling from one hand by their leather strap. His T-shirt, blotched with sweat, moulded onto the twin curves of his pecs.

"Hello, old friend!" he shouted.

So thrilling and familiar, the nearly forgotten timbre of his voice. And thrilling too the look in his eyes. A raw, new thing, suggesting insecurity and hope, presaging all that would unfold. Lovers, then spouses. Children. Shared success and failure. And, unmasked at last, our mature mutual affection.

This I recognize in hindsight. But that day, in my renewed apprehension, I wasn't so sure. For as he exited the shadow, he raked his long hair from his face with his fingers, and in the morning light his biceps knotted spectacularly.

A smile tugging the corners of my mouth, my breath whooshed out. I froze, rooted to the spot. *Oh, shit*, I said to myself as his arms enfolded me. *Not again!*

co-author's note

To fall in love with someone is also to fall in love with their story. For many gay men, this starts right away, over post-coital pillow talk. Sharing tales of the first time we each had sex with another man. Or when we finally came out to our families. Where we grew up. What it was like there for gay boys like us.

In this way, soon after Alex and I met he started wooing me with stories of his BC boyhood in the '50s and '60s. Driven by my growing affection for him, the places he spoke of took on almost mythical dimensions. The little house in Harrison Hot Springs, his family home on Lillooet Avenue for nearly sixty years. The beaches on Harrison Lake: Green Point and Sandy Cove. The majestic features dominating the Harrison and Fraser rivers: Bear Mountain, Mounts Cheam and Woodside, grandees of the Cascade and Lillooet ranges.

And his haunts in Vancouver—the old Vancouver School of Art with its odd faux-Egyptian pylon towering over the entrance, his first boarding house with its curmudgeonly landlady, the apartment house on West Seventh Avenue near Oak and its wild collection of college kids.

When he shared with me the drafts of the short stories he had been working on, I was moved to find all of the locations he had described lovingly detailed, along with the original models for this book's cast of characters.

There was the fixture at the West Seventh Avenue house, Doug Haddow, Alex's first love and the model for Ted's boyfriend, Marc. There was Alex's great unrequited love, Vern Barber, the progenitor of the novel's bad boy, Wade. And Alex's high school pal, Vicki Tyndall, the likely prototype for Ted's best friend Joanne. Lastly, there was Alex's housemate on the ground floor at West Seventh Avenue, the brilliant artist Michael Morris, the partial origin for the novel's Michael.

All gone now, save for the traces of them that remain in the pages of this book.

Gone too are Alex's stomping grounds in early '60s Vancouver. Though the seedy areas of Downtown Eastside remain magnets for shady behaviour, faded from memory are the dives of the city's burgeoning queer community, all experiencing their heydays back then. The Montreal Club, the Castle, and the queer-adjacent Smilin' Buddha. Vanished as well are Vancouver's iconic Aristocratic diners that once could be found throughout the city.

In addition to being a poignant story of personal development, *Confluence* contributes to our understanding of the little-described decade in queer Canadian history prior to the 1969 Stonewall Uprising—the event that sparked the modern gay rights movement.

During this period of enormous change, in Vancouver and the small Upper Fraser Valley towns, the conformist '50s were, as elsewhere, morphing into the politically divisive and freewheeling '60s.

As described in the novel's second part, in Vancouver the move toward acceptance of gay love and sexuality was sidelined in the broader push for sexual liberation. And the city's queer community—far from benefiting from the era's drive for civil rights—continued to suffer discrimination and police harassment.

Even so, Vancouver was a mecca for a new generation of queer people whose social networks and gathering places—albeit largely out of sight—became the foundation for the thriving LGBTQ+ culture that blossomed post-Stonewall.

The small towns of Harrison Hot Springs and Agassiz, though largely at the periphery of this cultural moment, were powerfully affected by it, nonetheless. Brought largely by returning sons and daughters—Alex among them—the new artistic influences and social practices, as well as the books and generation-defining music of the day, all made their way to these Upper Fraser Valley towns.

Although he was a successful visual artist and educator, it wasn't until 1998 that Alex began limning this era in earnest through his writing, heeding, after his retirement from teaching, the urgings of his favourite aunt—the writer and publicist Marjorie Gow.

Though Alex was well read, he lacked the confidence and skill to shape into a unified narrative the copious material he went on to generate for over nearly two decades. I have no doubt that given more time he would have remedied this, augmenting his scant formal training, as I have, through classes, critique groups, and mentorship.

Time, though, was something he did not have. Cancer and chemotherapy made it impossible for him to complete the novel, though he laboured on it until the spring of 2019, when he was required to leave home and enter palliative care.

At Toronto's Bridgepoint Hospital, ours was the largest room in the unit, a corner space with sweeping views out floor-to-ceiling windows. To the west was downtown Toronto, the spine of towers stacked along Yonge Street congregating at its intersection with Eglinton Avenue. To the north was Riverdale Park back-grounded by the steel curtain of the Bloor Viaduct, North York a shadow in the distance.

Those who have seen Brie Larson's Emmy Award–winning performance in the film *Room* (2015) will recognize these accommodations as the place where the protagonist and her son go to recuperate after their kidnapping and long captivity. For the characters, it was a liminal space, a place to heal before expanding into a life resumed. For us as well, it was a way station at the edge of the world—but a world Alex was preparing to leave behind.

And there one sunny afternoon, when he was still feeling lively and in good spirits, our conversation turned to his novel and his other unfinished artistic projects. He said, in his usual laconic way, "Looks like I won't be able to get to all that stuff."

He paused then, looked out the window where the boy in the movie had stood surveying his new world. There, the trees had almost finished leafing out in the park where people ran on the track or played soccer in the game fields. Breaking the silence at last, he said, "I guess you'll have to do it."

I smiled wanly when he returned his attention to me. But, stunned by the remark, I was unable to shape my thoughts into a response. As the months after his death progressed, though, I realized that in that silence I made a promise, one that drew me toward the unusual project of completing his novel.

As I read through Alex's unfinished stories, I was struck by the depth with which he wrote about the mores of Vancouver's gay enclave and the small Upper Fraser Valley towns, the humour and poetic language, the sweep of his decade-long narrative. And the work's inventive structure: the novel-in-stories.

The novel-in-stories is a form I love, having employed it myself in my debut work, *Dreaming Home* (Biblioasis, 2023). Similar to my novel, *Confluence* is composed of eight short stories. Each tale has its own arc, but one that contributes to the overarching narrative of a small-town boy—his family, friends, and lovers—and his unrequited affection for his mercurial best friend.

When I began editing his material, I found it in need of considerable shaping. However, his eight existing stories—in addition to his memoiristic writings—provided an excellent structure on which the novel could grow. It was a method that came to me quite naturally, having employed it in converting my own previously published short stories into *Dreaming Home*.

Though in need of reorganization, three among Alex's original tales were sound. One other lay outside the novel's overarching narrative but could, with some effort, be adapted to flesh out the protagonist's early-twenties life in Vancouver. As for the remaining stories, they required of me something akin to archaeology—sifting through hundreds of drafts to identify and sharpen the structure toward which Alex had been driving.

Though the story is entirely his, as well as much of the words, many changes were necessary to fulfill the novel's promise. Bridging information was added to the beginnings of tales since at the time of his death Alex had not realized his plan to unify the material. Important moments in the novel needed expanding to maximize their effect. Some new scenes were added utilizing text and incidents gleaned from his editorial notes, letters, and memoiristic writings, as well as personal anecdotes and photographs from the period.

The opening chapters, which were previously written in a young-adult style, were synchronized with the rest of the manuscript's more reflective, literary approach. Lastly, the language in any manuscript, no matter how excellent, needs refinement. I have done so here, as with all my modifications, by challenging myself to remain true to his voice and intent.

Given these many interventions, the resulting manuscript can now be properly understood as a work of joint authorship. Though *Confluence* foremostly asks to be read and appreciated on its artistic merits, that enjoyment may be deepened by understanding its place in the tradition of queer literary collaboration and legacy-making.

On the generative side, one prominent example is that of lovers Gertrude Stein and Alice B. Toklas whose formal collaboration resulted in *The Autobiography of Alice B. Toklas*, where a blended voice and editorial curatorship yielded a foundational work of queer literature.

Likewise, romantic partners Monique Wittig and Sande Zeig exemplify this intellectual collaboration. Their co-produced works include *Lesbian Peoples: Material for a Dictionary*, a hybrid work of queer theory, and the feminist film noir *The Girl*.

Confluence's act of literary stewardship and legacy extension is also part of a rich queer tradition.

One precedent spanning several generations is that of E.M. Forster, Christopher Isherwood, and Don Bachardy. Though not romantic partners, Forster became Isherwood's literary mentor and was profoundly supportive of the younger man, both professionally and personally. In turn, Isherwood became a steward of Forster's literary legacy by helping to shape and publish Forster's seminal queer novel, *Maurice*, and by writing its introduction.

Isherwood's own legacy was stewarded by his partner of over thirty years, Don Bachardy, whose input on Isherwood's literary projects during his lifetime became deep curatorial oversight after his death in the publication of Isherwood's diaries.

One can find this same legacy stewardship in the case of Truman Capote, through the efforts of his partner of thirty-five years, Jack Dunphy—the 1987 *Dear Genius: A Memoir of My Life with Truman Capote* and through his management of Capote's estate.

Similarly, the professional life of the American writer Paul Monette was transformed by the loss of his mate, Roger Horwitz. Shifting from lighter work, Monette went on to become the chronicler of love and loss during the AIDS crisis through his memorializing of Horwitz in *Borrowed Time: An AIDS Memoir* and the collection of poetry *Love Alone: Eighteen Elegies for Rog*. These works mirror broader, queer community–based memorial and legacy efforts at that time such as the AIDS Memorial Quilt, which began as a small San Francisco–based project and went on to become a worldwide phenomenon.

Placed in this context, *Confluence* can be seen not merely as an editorial artifact—one author's reshaping of another author's work—but rather, as a genuine blending of literary sensibilities, a voice unified through the shared experience of two spouses, who lived and worked closely together. It is at once, then, an act of legacy extension, a twinned artistic expression, and a manifestation of a deep and abiding love.

For this, I am grateful beyond all measure. That Alex and I are still together, labouring these many years after his death to create something of meaning and beauty. Gratified that his personal journey, on which these stories are based, will now be more widely known. Delighted, as well, that we've rescued from oblivion such a dynamic time and place.

Lucian Childs
February 1, 2026
Toronto, Ontario

acknowledgments

My thanks go out to long-time Harrison Hot Springs residents Dan and Lynda Scobie for fact-checking earlier versions of the manuscript. Dan, a former tree faller, offered invaluable insight into the logging industry around Harrison Lake in the '50s and '60s.

I am indebted as well to Nadine Gairns, Alex's childhood friend, for reviewing the text and commenting on her and Alex's shared experience at Agassiz High School.

My heart goes out to Patricia Tolmie, Alex's niece, who offered insight and incident that informed the characters based on Alex's parents, Sam and Bess Turner.

The friends from Alex's foundational period in Vancouver have many times over earned my thanks: Diane Dryden, Robert Wallace, Dick Wey. Also deserving my gratitude are his Toronto friends from his years teaching at the Art Centre of the Central Technical School: Sheryl Dudley, Evangeline Wong, Dawn and Doug Hemmy, Chris Kudryk, Joel Masewich, Peter Vietgen. And our dear friends Cindy Church, Rosa Quintana-Lilo and Mike Edwards, Henry Wright and Richard Davidson, who have followed this project at each step.

My gratitude goes out as well to the staff of the non-profits Alex long supported: Raegan Swanson, executive director, The ArQuives; Beth Clarke, executive director, Wilderness Committee; Dena Ellery, donor relations manager, Wilderness Committee; Andy Hillhouse, executive and artistic director, Harrison Festival Society.

I am beholden to the Canadian literary journals *The New Quarterly* and *Prairie Fire* for agreeing to the unusual request to posthumously publish chapters of this work. I am indebted as well to the writers Caroline Adderson and Trevor Corkum for weighing in on earlier drafts of the manuscript. And to the late Nancy Zafris for her early tough love and encouragement. I am ever in awe of these writers' craft and discernment, both in their own work and in the assistance they have provided me over the years.

I am indebted to the great folks at Arsenal Pulp Press for including me in key creative decisions. Publisher Brian Lam, editors JC Cham and Catharine Chen, publicists Cynara Geissler and Erin Chan. My profound gratitude goes to the talented book designer Jazmin Welch, who went above and beyond in this book's preparation and whose collaborative spirit included me in every step of the design process.

Writing is such a solitary endeavour. While I had the melancholy sweetness of this story wrung from Alex's life to accompany me, I was heartened during the long editorial process to be supported by my writing group—Ken Harvey, Lee Parpart, Ariane Blackman, Stephanie Eng, Renée Sgroi, and Ed Seaward—and by my many friends.

Since this is a book about adolescence and homecoming, I would be remiss if I did not thank my sister, Missy McCarroll, and my friend Betty Pong, who for almost twenty-five years has provided Alex and me with our lovely Toronto home.

Lastly, my deepest gratitude goes to Alex himself. Our love remains an abiding presence—the bedrock of all my creative work.

ALEX TURNER was born in Vancouver in 1940, his parents having met the previous year at Locarno Beach, where his father worked as a lifeguard. In 1953, Alex and his family relocated to a small house in Harrison Hot Springs, where, after graduating from Agassiz High School, he spent his summers for the next fifty-seven years. With degrees from the Vancouver School of Art (now Emily Carr University of Art + Design) and the University of British Columbia, Alex taught in Toronto at the Art Centre of the Central Technical School. Until his death in 2019, he maintained his artistic practice, exhibiting work in Ontario and British Columbia. Encouraged by a favourite aunt—an author and publicist—to write short stories, Alex turned his attention to fiction after his retirement from teaching. His short fiction has appeared in the Canadian literary journals *The New Quarterly* and *Prairie Fire*. *Confluence* is his debut novel. For more about his work, please visit ***alexjturner.ca***.

LUCIAN CHILDS is a fiction writer whose debut novel, *Dreaming Home* (Biblioasis, 2023), won the Fred Kerner Book Award and was shortlisted for the Rakuten Kobo Emerging Writer Prize in literary fiction. He was a Peter Taylor Fellow at the Kenyon Review Writers Workshop, a recipient of the Rasmuson Foundation Individual Artist Project Award, and a finalist for the Faulkner-Wisdom Short Story Award. He is a contributing editor of the 2017 Lambda Literary Award finalist *Building Fires in the Snow: a collection of Alaska* LGBTQ *short fiction and poetry*. His stories, essays, and reviews have appeared on WritersDigest.com and in the literary journals *Grain*, *Plenitude*, *The Ex-Puritan*, and *Prairie Fire*, among others. Originally from Dallas, Texas, he resides in Toronto, Ontario. For more about his work, please visit ***lucianchilds.com***.

◀ *Alex Turner (left) and Lucian Childs*